Her kiss was a tender expression of gratitude...

But Preston's reaction to it was fierce and swift. He pulled her close and deepened the kiss. She didn't resist. Giving in to temptation, she melted into him.

With each heartbeat, his touch became rougher, his kiss burned hotter. Then to her complete surprise, he eased his hold.

Abby looked into his eyes and saw the iron-willed control he held over himself.

"I'm sorry," she said. "You didn't start this, and I can see you don't want to..."

"I don't *want* to?" He laughed, a dark, edgy sound. "I want you, Abby. I care about you more than I should. But you need to be protected—even from me."

"You want me..." she said slowly, savoring the words. "Then show me."

Dear Harlequin Intrigue Reader,

For nearly thirty years fearless romance has fueled every Harlequin Intrigue book. Now we want everyone to know about the great crime stories our fantastic authors write and the variety of compelling miniseries we offer. We think our new cover look complements and enhances our promise to deliver edge-of-your-seat reads in all six of our titles—and brand-new titles every month!

This month's lineup is packed with nonstop mystery in *Smoky Ridge Curse,* the third in Paula Graves's Bitterwood P.D. trilogy, exciting action in *Sharpshooter,* the next installment in Cynthia Eden's Shadow Agents miniseries, and of course fearless romance—whether from newcomers Jana DeLeon and HelenKay Dimon or veteran author Aimée Thurlo, we've got every angle covered.

Next month buckle up as Debra Webb returns with a new Colby Agency series featuring The Specialists. And in November *USA TODAY* bestselling author B.J. Daniels takes us back to "The Canyon" for her special *Christmas at Cardwell Ranch* celebration.

Lots going on and lots more to come. Be sure to check out www.Harlequin.com for what's coming next.

Enjoy,

Denise Zaza

Senior Editor

Harlequin Intrigue

FALCON'S RUN

—

AIMÉE THURLO

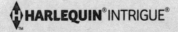

Recycling programs for this product may not exist in your area.

With special thanks to Doug Baum and Dr. Steve Komadina, who shared with me so much of their time and expertise about camels.

ISBN-13: 978-0-373-69709-0

FALCON'S RUN

Copyright © 2013 by Aimée and David Thurlo

All rights reserved. Except for use in any review, the reproduction or utilization of this work in whole or in part in any form by any electronic, mechanical or other means, now known or hereafter invented, including xerography, photocopying and recording, or in any information storage or retrieval system, is forbidden without the written permission of the publisher, Harlequin Enterprises Limited, 225 Duncan Mill Road, Don Mills, Ontario M3B 3K9, Canada.

This is a work of fiction. Names, characters, places and incidents are either the product of the author's imagination or are used fictitiously, and any resemblance to actual persons, living or dead, business establishments, events or locales is entirely coincidental.

This edition published by arrangement with Harlequin Books S.A.

For questions and comments about the quality of this book, please contact us at CustomerService@Harlequin.com.

® and TM are trademarks of Harlequin Enterprises Limited or its corporate affiliates. Trademarks indicated with ® are registered in the United States Patent and Trademark Office, the Canadian Trade Marks Office and in other countries.

Printed in U.S.A.

ABOUT THE AUTHOR

Aimée Thurlo is a nationally known bestselling author. She's the winner of a Career Achievement Award from *RT Book Reviews,* a New Mexico Book Award in contemporary fiction and a Willa Cather Award in the same category. Her novels have been published in twenty countries worldwide.

She also cowrites the bestselling Ella Clah mainstream mystery series praised in the *New York Times Book Review*.

Aimée was born in Havana, Cuba, and lives with her husband of thirty-nine years in Corrales, New Mexico. Her husband, David, was raised on a Navajo Indian reservation.

Books by Aimée Thurlo

HARLEQUIN INTRIGUE
 988—COUNCIL OF FIRE‡
1011—RESTLESS WIND‡
1064—STARGAZER'S WOMAN‡
1154—NAVAJO COURAGE‡
1181—THE SHADOW‡
1225—ALPHA WARRIOR‡
1253—TWILIGHT WARRIOR*
1316—WINTER HAWK'S LEGEND**
1333—POWER OF THE RAVEN**
1394—SECRETS OF THE LYNX**
1442—FALCON'S RUN**

‡Brotherhood of Warriors
*Long Mountain Heroes
**Copper Canyon

CAST OF CHARACTERS

Preston Bowman—The Hartley police detective lives for his job—that is, until he meets the beautiful owner of Sitting Tall Ranch, a riding facility for special-needs kids. Preston vows to find a killer so she can reopen her doors, but time is working against him on every front.

Abby Langdon—She created Sitting Tall Ranch as a memorial to her twin sister. Now she stands to lose it all—along with the police detective who has captured her heart.

Kyle Goodluck—An NCIS agent on leave, he's suddenly thrown into his foster brother Preston's investigation and attempt to catch a killer.

Stan Cooper—He's Abby's business adviser and accountant. Stan's trying desperately to help her stay in the black, but the numbers aren't adding up right.

"Lightning" Rod Garner—Charismatic despite his explosive temper, he's Abby and the ranch's staunchest ally.

Ilse Sheridan—Not only is she singularly attractive, Ilse is also Rod Garner's assistant and top adviser. Ilse has an MBA and no life beyond her career, but she has her own dreams, too, ones she keeps a secret from all but her one friend.

Daniel Hawk—His loyalty to his brother is absolute and he'll stand beside Preston, bringing all the assets of his security company into play, until the killer's caught.

Bobby Neskahi—The ten-year-old foster child has juvenile arthritis and an indomitable spirit. Most of what he sees and hears are products of his imagination, like the story about his father the spy, but his near photographic memory is an asset no one can ignore.

Chapter One

Armed with her favorite guilty pleasure—a caramel vanilla cappuccino—Abby Langdon left Sunny Perk in the distance and navigated the long gravel road that led to her ranch. Later, she'd put on a pot of coffee, but for now, her fix was complete.

Already she was anticipating the hard work and long day ahead. Sitting Tall Ranch and its special mission had always been her dream come true. Young victims of illness, poverty and abuse came to her ranch daily for a respite from their challenges. Her guests had witnessed the worst life could hand out, but Sitting Tall Ranch was the haven where they could forget their troubles and just be kids.

Abby slowed as she neared the abandoned pickup parked alongside the road. She'd seen it earlier when she'd left the ranch. Somebody had probably run out of gas then gotten a ride.

Abby drove through the gates, parked and headed to her office, a separate *casita* behind the main house. She was holding her to-go cup in one hand and reaching for her keys with the other when she heard a familiar voice to her left.

"Abby! Wait up!"

Ten-year-old Bobby Neskahi, hands down her favorite guest, was struggling up the sidewalk. Juvenile rheumatoid arthritis had damaged most of his joints and left him to rely on braces, but whatever had caused the panicked look on his face was urging him to move fast.

He stopped in front of her, catching his breath. "Carl's hurt! He's not moving."

"Where is he?" Her heart suddenly beat overtime. Carl Woods was her caretaker, animal handler and all-around right-hand man on the ranch.

"He's inside Tracker and Missy's turnout area. He's on the ground, and he didn't move or answer when I called him." Bobby grabbed her hand. "He might be dead. I couldn't see him breathing. Come on! You gotta help!"

Abby touched Bobby firmly on the shoulder, then handed him her keys. "Bobby, I need you to go into my office, call 911 on the desk phone, then stay here until the police arrive. You'll have to show them the way. I'll go check on Carl."

Bobby nodded and Abby took off running toward the stalls.

Jogging around the corner of the barn, Abby nearly collided with a wheelbarrow stacked with bales of alfalfa hay. Stopping just in time, she began inching between the wheelbarrow and the fence. Out of the corner of her eye she caught a glimpse of movement.

As she turned to look, a large figure leaped up from behind the stack and forced an empty feed bag over her head.

"Hey!" Sputtering from the debris in her eyes and mouth, she fought to pull the bag off.

Strong arms grabbed her wrists, yanked them down to her sides, then lifted her off the ground.

Abby tried to kick her captor, but he just grunted, hauled her several steps, then flung her violently onto the ground.

DARK, ANGRY CLOUDS were building over Copper Canyon. "Storm's heading our way." Hot from exertion despite the cool, early hour, Detective Preston Bowman had already shrugged off his shirt as he continued working alongside his brother, repairing gaps in the fence line. Their late foster father's place belonged to all of them now.

As the wind from the downdrafts intensified, Preston could feel the force of the approaching storm. The sky continued to darken quickly, turning the new day into near twilight.

Kyle, taller than his brother by one inch and just as muscular, wiped his eyes with a dirty hand. "Rain I like. Sandstorms, not so much, bro."

Preston was tired, though he'd never admit it. His sore muscles were a constant reminder of why he'd chosen city life instead. As a cop, Preston was more used to wielding a gun rather than a shovel, axe or sledgehammer. Even though he was six feet tall and in excellent shape—police work demanded it—he was ready for a break.

Kyle reached for his shirt. "I'd forgotten what it feels like to be sandblasted."

"Have you decided if you're going to be coming home for good?" Preston grabbed his own shirt and ducked inside the toolshed.

"Not yet," Kyle said, joining him in the small shelter. "I have some things to work out first." He shook his head and shrugged. "Can't say anything else—classified."

Preston nodded silently. He didn't have to know the details to realize whatever it was had hit Kyle like a hard kick to his gut. Despite that, he knew his brother would find a way to deal with it.

Inside each of his five brothers was a fighter who never gave up. They'd all been tested at an early age, long before they'd even known how to protect themselves from life's hard knocks.

Their stories were all different but shared the same core. They'd been wards of the state, abandoned by people who were supposed to have protected and loved them. Survival instincts had become second nature to each of them early on.

When life did its best to bring them to their knees, they got up and kept fighting. It was what they did best. The difference was now they had each other's backs. Though none of them were bound by blood, their pasts had forged unbreakable ties among them.

A flash of lightning was followed immediately by an ear-splitting crack of thunder that shook the ground. Hearing a horse's panicked whinny, Kyle shot out of the shed and ran toward the corral. "Red!"

The large mahogany horse with the dark mane was bucking wildly, racing around the corral and tossing his head.

"Red's used to his own stall inside Gene's barn. He doesn't like it here," Kyle said.

Preston took the horse by its halter, led him to the side of the house and stood there with him. "He'll settle down now that he's here with us, sheltered from the wind," he said. "How come Red's here? Did Gene loan him to you for a few days?"

"No. He's donating him to Sitting Tall Ranch. The owner, Abby Langdon, was looking for a gentle mount for kids with special needs. Red's steady as they come—except around thunder. If he's inside a barn, he's okay, but not if he's outside. Since I'd planned on keeping him here for a day or two so I could go riding, I checked the weather ahead of time. It was supposed to be okay, just a little cloudy, but this front's a day early."

As they stood waiting for the storm to pass, Preston kept his arm over the horse's neck. The animal seemed to be handling things better now.

"Have you opened the envelope *Hosteen* Silver left for you yet?" Preston asked, referring to their foster father.

"No, not yet. He knew things before they happened and that always spooked me. There's also something else I need to take into account now. After Daniel, Gene and Paul opened theirs, they ended up getting married within months. I'm thinking that I'll hold on to mine for another decade or so," he said and flashed his brother a quick grin.

Preston laughed. "Just so you know, they're not all letters that foretell upcoming events. Mine's a sketch." Preston reached for his wallet and took out a folded piece of paper. "I made a copy to keep with me until I figured it out."

"Nice. The old man was a good artist, though he seldom had time for that," Kyle said, studying it. "That's obviously Copper Canyon and there's Falcon. It looks just like the fetish he gave you when you turned sixteen."

"I've carried that carving with me every day since," Preston said, lifting the leather cord that hung around his neck. A small leather pouch hung from it. "Falcon's a faithful spiritual guide. I think he helps me see what others miss. That's a great asset in police work."

"In the sketch, Falcon's swooping down on that owl and defending something…a nest or maybe its mate? The background's mostly in shadow and hard to make out. Can you see it any better in the original?"

"No, not even enlarged."

"What's that drifting down?" Kyle asked, pointing. "A gray feather?"

"Feather, yes, but in the original, it's blue."

"*Hosteen* Silver used to say that blue jays, or piñon jays as he called them, stood for peace and happiness," Kyle said. "So was he saying that you'll be so busy fighting you'll miss out on happiness?"

"Your guess is as good as mine," Preston answered.

Kyle shook his head. "Everything about that man was mysterious. Even his name. *Hosteen* means mister. Silver was a nickname given to him because of his long silver hair."

Noting the wind had calmed down and things were returning to normal, Preston started leading the horse back to the corral. Just then a big barn owl flew out of the pine tree beside him. The bird swooped past him with a faint rustle of feathers, then turned sharply and angled up toward the cliff, disappearing into the background of rocks and brush.

Preston led the horse away quickly, grateful that Red had seemed oblivious to the owl and was now back to his usual calm self. His one fear—thunder—had subsided.

"The worst is over," Preston said.

"Not by a long shot, bro. *You're* the falcon in the drawing, and that was an owl we both saw swooping down out of that pine. For you, it's just starting."

Before he could reply, Preston's phone rang. He turned the reins over to his brother, gesturing for him to put the horse away, and answered the call.

Mere minutes later he met Kyle, who was standing by the department's SUV. Preston had changed shirts and was ready to go. "I need to race over to Hartley. I'm the closest cop and some kid just reported what he thinks is a dead body at Sitting Tall Ranch."

"Watch your back, bro. Looks like things are already in motion."

Preston slipped inside the SUV, then glanced out the window, his face hard, his gaze deadly. "Whatever's coming will find me ready and waiting."

Chapter Two

As Abby fell, her head hit something hard. Dizzying flashes of light exploded before her eyes, and for a moment she lay dazed and unable to move.

Her attacker grabbed her under her arms, dragged her several feet, then dropped her to the ground again. Disoriented, she waited for several long moments, hearing the fading sound of heavy footsteps.

Slowly regaining her wits, Abby sat up, tugged the bag off her head and looked around, trying to get her bearings and cope with the dull ache radiating from her head. She was in the stall prepared for the new horse, Big Red, who was due to arrive in a day or so. Both upper and lower stall doors were closed, but light still filtered in.

Abby listened for a moment, looking around. She was alone, and with the exception of the sound of horses moving about in the nearby stalls, snorting and anxious to be fed, she could hear nothing unusual.

Still cautious, she pushed the door. It was latched from the outside and wouldn't budge, and both sections of the Dutch door had been connected with outside barrel bolts, so she couldn't go under or over by opening just one. Peeking through the narrow gap, she saw where the metal latch had been lowered into the catch. Somehow she'd need to raise the big pin about an inch.

Abby peered around her, hoping to find a piece of baling wire she could work between the door and jamb. Unfortunately, she also had a safety rule requiring that no baling
wire or metal objects be left on the ground where an animal
could get tangled or cut up.

Poking through the hay debris, she noticed that one of the
heavy wire tines of the metal feeder bolted to the wall had
broken away from the weld at the bottom and could be twisted
loose. That was what she needed. Thirty seconds later she
managed to work the latch free, and the door swung open.

Abby hurried outside. Nobody was around. The horses in
the pen ahead were moving about nervously, and when she
drew closer, she saw Carl lying facedown on the ground by
the feeder.

Hank, one of their two resident camels, was in the adjoin-
ing turnout. When he saw her, he roared loudly, the distressed
sound reminding her of Chewbacca in *Star Wars*.

"Carl?" Abby scaled the fence and ran over. As she bent
down for a closer look, she saw that the back of his head was
a wet mass of tissue and blood. No one could have survived
that kind of head injury. Outrage and sorrow gripped her.

Abby was struggling for breath when she heard a car door
slam in the distance. Wondering if the attacker could have
been the driver of the pickup parked on the road, Abby raced
uphill. If she could read the license plate, she'd be able to give
the police something solid to go on.

Once at the top, Abby saw the pickup and rushed out onto
the road for a closer look. That was a mistake. The driver
spun the truck around and accelerated, coming straight at her.

Abby stared at the darkened windshield, frozen in terror.
The driver's face was lost to her, but his intent to kill her
was clear.

Just then a dark SUV with flashing lights came racing over
the hill—a response to Bobby's 911.

The SUV swerved left, cut around her, then slid to a stop between her and the oncoming truck.

The pickup quickly returned to its lane, then sped past the SUV and continued over the hill.

An officer wearing a dark Hartley police jacket stepped out of the SUV. As Abby went to thank him, her knees buckled.

He was there in an instant, his arms secure around her waist and holding her gently against him. "Hang on, ma'am. I'll call an ambulance. Your head's injured."

"No, I'm fine," she said quickly, stepping back to stand on her own. She touched the emerging bump on her forehead. At least she wasn't bleeding.

Abby looked up at him, straight into the darkest eyes she'd ever seen. His steady gaze was like the man himself—strong and hard—a rock to lean on. "You just saved my life."

"I'm Detective Preston Bowman of the Hartley P.D. You're safe now," he said, his voice calm and reassuring.

For a moment she felt tempted to step right back into his arms and rest against his hard chest. To forget…

She drew in a sharp breath. "I'm Abby Langdon. You need to come down to the ranch right away. Something's happened to Carl Woods, my head trainer," she said, telling him everything in a short burst.

"Let's go," he said, hurrying back to his SUV with her. "Hop in."

"This whole thing…it feels like a nightmare…but it's real," she whispered, closing the passenger-side door.

"All I caught was glare off the glass. Did you see the driver's face or his license plate?" he asked, easing down the hill, then making the turn into the long driveway.

"No, but it wasn't for lack of trying," she said.

"All right then. I called it in as soon as he took off. We'll see what happens now. I've heard of what you do here, Abby. Now tell me more about your animal handler."

"He's…" Her voice broke and she brushed away a tear. If she started crying now, would she ever stop? She took a deep breath and held it together.

He pulled up in front of the logs anchored in place to serve as a parking barrier. "Just point me in the right direction. This is a police matter and I'll handle it."

His steady voice and calm confidence made it easier for her to trust him. He'd stepped into an unpredictable situation and had taken charge effortlessly, as if it was second nature to him. Something assured her that Detective Bowman was very good at his job.

They climbed out of the SUV, and she led him quickly to the turnout area alongside the barn. As they approached, she saw that Bobby had left her office and was now standing just outside the welded pipe enclosure where Carl lay.

"I need to get Bobby away from there," she said quickly. "He's too young to deal with things like this and he's seen too much already."

"Bobby's your son?" he asked, noting that the boy was Navajo.

"No, he's always my first guest of the day. He's also one of my regular helpers," she said. "He found Carl and made the 911 call. Is it okay if I go take care of him?"

"Yeah. This is no place for a kid. Find a place where he can stay, just make sure he doesn't leave the property. He may have seen or heard something that could help us."

As Abby hurried to the boy, she could see Carl's body in her periphery. A silent scream rose inside her, filling her mind and nearly obliterating her ability to think.

"He's…dead, isn't he?" Bobby whispered.

He seemed remarkably controlled considering the circumstances. But she'd seen that same look on other faces before and recognized it for what it was. Many would mistake it for indifference, but fear, the kind that clung with razor-sharp tentacles to your soul, often mimicked bravery. She remembered seeing it in her twin sister's eyes as treatment after treatment had failed to cure her.

Taking a deep breath and forcing herself to focus on the present, Abby turned her head and saw Detective Bowman had ducked through the gap in the welded pipe fence. He had latex gloves on and was now crouched next to Carl's body. After checking for Carl's pulse, he looked up and shook his head, affirming what she already knew.

Abby focused on Bobby. "We need to leave. Other officers and medical people will be here soon and will need us to point the way back here."

Bobby didn't move, his gaze still locked on Carl. "Do you think Missy or Tracker kicked him?" he asked in a thin voice.

She hadn't even considered that possibility until now. "I can't imagine either of those horses hurting anyone. They're the calmest animals I've ever known. I've never seen either of them spook, not under any circumstances," she said, taking an unsteady breath. Somehow her voice had remained steady but her hands were shaking badly. Not wanting Bobby to see that, she jammed them into her pockets. "Carl was their trainer and the animals knew and liked him. They never even flinched or pulled away when he cleaned their hooves. There's no way they hurt him."

"Then who did this?"

Abby drew in another unsteady breath. "I don't know, Bobby. That's what Detective Bowman is here to find out." She tried to urge Bobby along, but he refused to move.

"I'm going to miss Carl, Abby. He was my friend and I don't have that many. The kids at the foster home play a lot of football and baseball, but I can't. Carl liked the same kind of games I do. We'd pretend we were spies and do a lot of cool stuff." A tear trickled down one cheek, but he brushed it away instantly.

She wanted to give him a hug, but she knew Bobby would think she was babying him and would hate that. "It's okay to be sad. I am, too, Bobby."

He nodded but didn't answer her directly, avoiding the subject altogether. "The detective's Navajo, like me. Did you notice? He has to work around the body and that's dangerous, but he knows how to protect himself so he'll stay safe," he said. "See that leather bag on the cord around his neck? That's not jewelry, and he's not just trying to look Indian. That bag protects him."

"From what? I don't understand," Abby said.

"Spirits stick around and like making trouble for people. Mrs. Nez—she cooks for us back at the foster home—told me that," he said.

Abby hesitated, unsure what to say. "Carl would never hurt either one of us, not when he was alive or now that he's passed on," she said. "Bobby, you may not need a hug, but I do." She bent down and held him. As she did, Abby felt the tremor that shook his small body.

After a moment she stepped away and Bobby refused to look at her, almost as if embarrassed. "Tell the detective that I followed the rule of three, okay?"

"The what?"

"He'll know," he said. "We better go. The sirens are coming closer."

She nodded. "You're right. We'll need to stay out of everyone's way."

They walked back up the path away from the barn and the enclosures. Abby set a slow pace, but not so much that Bobby would think she was deferring to him. Bobby faced many difficulties daily, but he had a lot of pride, something that helped him endure.

Hearing Hank the camel roar loudly, Abby halted. "Bobby, go ahead without me. Make sure the other officers and emergency people know where to find the detective. I need to get the horses out of the turnout area and move Hank to another pen so the police can work in peace."

"Okay, but if you get scared or something, shout out or whistle. I'll hear you."

"Thanks," Abby said and smiled. Bobby was as loyal as could be. It was one of the many reasons she was so fond of him.

Abby jogged back to where she'd left the detective. Though the horses were clearly upset by the stranger in their enclosure, they were still acting in a predictable manner. Both stood as far away from Detective Bowman as possible, at the innermost corner of the enclosure, watching him, their ears pinned back.

"Detective, let me put halters on the horses and lead them to another pen. They'll be out of your way then."

"No, stay put. This is a crime scene," he said. "I see a hoof pick over there and a coffee can with some traces of grain. I'll dump that out then check their hooves, scrape off any dirt and debris into the can and then bring them out to you."

Preston looked around for a rope and halter but, finding neither within arm's reach, decided to forego using them. He bent down and checked each of Missy's hooves. Using the pick, he collected dirt and what could be blood and hair. Once finished, he grabbed the mare by the mane and led her over to Abby, who immediately opened the small turnout gate.

"You know horses," Abby said.

"Yeah. It was part of life where I grew up."

Abby grabbed Missy's mane as he'd done and led her out to another corral. By the time she returned, Detective Bowman was waiting with Tracker.

Abby grabbed the horse but as her gaze strayed to Carl, a lump formed at her throat. How could this have happened? Nothing made sense to her anymore.

"Was he a close friend?" Preston asked, as if sensing the turmoil inside her.

"We weren't close, but I considered him a friend. He was a good, loyal employee and a man who'd believed in my dream for Sitting Tall Ranch." She wanted to keep her voice steady, so she paused for a moment. "Do you know how…he died?" she added in a strained whisper.

"Not yet, but I'll find out. You can count on that."

Detective Bowman walked away from her and crouched by Carl's body once again. This time he looked around slowly, taking in the setting, not the victim. Although the gesture had seemed almost casual, she had a feeling he didn't miss much. Then, surprisingly, he looked back at her. His gaze was penetrating…and unsettling. She wanted to look away but somehow couldn't quite manage it.

To her, he represented the unknown…and that scared her. Would he be an ally, or would his appearance mark the last days of Sitting Tall Ranch? She'd made her mistakes—well-meaning ones, but if they came out now… Determined to guard her secrets, she moved away.

"We'll be blocking off several areas with yellow tape," he called out while taking photos with a small camera. "It may take a day or two before we're ready to take the tape down, so be prepared."

She tried not to give in to the unadulterated panic rising inside her. This wasn't just about Carl, not anymore. If the ranch became synonymous with danger, no parent would want their kids here. She'd lose her funding and have to shut down.

Sitting Tall Ranch was a place of healing and hope. There was no other place like it in the area. What they offered kids was something worth fighting for, and she intended to do whatever was necessary to keep the ranch's doors open.

"I'm going to need access to the animals," she said as Hank

let out another loud bellow. "Please try to keep that in mind when you put up the tape."

"No problem. I've got you covered."

"And please," she said softly, "work quickly. We need donations to survive, and with the economy, those have become harder and harder to get."

"You need closure, too, and finding answers is what I do best," he said. "Trust me."

She looked at him and blinked. She normally hated it when anyone said that. The words were usually empty and, if anything, meant she should do exactly the opposite. Yet there was something about Detective Bowman that assured her he was as good as his word.

Hearing another vehicle approaching, he turned his head to look, then glanced back at her. "Here comes Joanna Medina, the medical investigator," he said. "I'll need to speak to you and the boy as soon as I can, and when I do I'll let you know what we've found."

"Okay, thanks," she said. "I'm going to move Hank, the camel that's being so vocal right now. After that I'll be in my office, the *casita* behind the main house."

"One more thing," he called out to her. "The kid, Bobby, he didn't move or touch the body, right?"

"No, I think he would have been afraid to. He told me to tell you he'd followed the rule of three. He said you'd know what that meant."

Preston nodded. "Don't touch them, don't look at them, get away from them."

"The ghosts of the dead—that's the source of worry, right?" she asked.

"Not exactly," he said, meeting her outside the corral. "The *chindi* is the evil side of a man that remains earthbound waiting for a chance to create problems for the living. Our traditionalists believe that contact with the dead or their possessions is a sure way to draw it to you."

"You're an officer, so you're not…a traditionalist?"

"I'm a detective who does his job," he said, waving at a woman wearing a lab coat and carrying a heavy-looking medical case. "I have to get to work now. I'll come find you once we're through here and we can talk about what you saw before I got here."

As he strode away, a cold shudder ripped through Abby. She'd known anger, worry, love and ultimately loss. Yet she could count on one hand the times she'd experienced pure, unadulterated fear. Now as she watched the detective meet the medical examiner, she felt its icy-cold touch clawing into her again.

Carl was dead, and someone had attacked her here twice. No matter how hard she wished it wasn't so, the truth was that the ranch was no longer a safe haven.

Trying not to look back at Carl's body as she passed by, Abby returned to the pen that held Hank. Sensing that she was upset, the tall, gawky but somehow elegant animal nuzzled against her.

"Come on, old friend." She placed a halter on him, opened the gate and led him away.

As she walked, tears gathered but she blinked them away. She wouldn't fall apart now. She'd do what had to be done. Carl had shared her dream. He'd loved what they did here at the ranch daily: giving kids a chance to be kids again. He would have expected her to fight to keep it alive.

One way or another she'd see to it that Sitting Tall Ranch weathered the approaching storm.

Chapter Three

Preston considered the information he'd already gathered while the medical examiner worked. At first glance it had looked like an accident, a trampling death, but there were some inconsistencies. The wound to the back of the victim's skull showed no trace of sand, something sure to have been left by a horse's hoof, especially in this churned-up stall.

There also weren't any deep impressions or hoof marks near the body that would indicate the vic had been trampled. In fact, the only fresh prints near the body appeared to be from the vic's own boots.

He'd seen plenty of cowboys injured by horses at rodeos, but the way Carl's body lay seemed posed somehow. A cowboy kicked by a horse usually landed askew, not neatly on his face with arms laid out flat by his side. The fact that someone else had been on the premises and had attacked Abby, then tried to run her down, supported the likelihood of foul play.

That's when he'd taken another look at the ground by the body and discovered that someone had methodically obliterated the footprints along a strip of ground leading to and from the enclosure's gate. It had been skillfully done, but Preston was an experienced tracker and had spotted the signs.

Dr. Joanna Medina glanced up from the body. She was in her late fifties, with short silver hair and blue eyes that looked world weary and a little sad.

"You were right. This wasn't an accident. The wound on his head appears to have come from a blunt object. There's a second bruise on his chest, too. It's elongated, as if made by a stick or shovel." Joanna stood and handed him a clear plastic evidence bag. "Here's everything I found in the vic's pockets."

"Do you have a time of death for me?"

"All the markers tell me he died last night between nine and midnight."

As she prepared the body for transport, Preston, still wearing gloves to avoid fingerprint contamination, studied the vic's possessions. There was a small notepad with feeding schedules, a ranch staff ID and a wallet with five bucks but no driver's license. Because there was no metro bus service and only one cab company around, it was unusual for locals not to have a license. He'd ask Abby about it.

As he walked back, Preston glanced over at the parking area and saw that the ranch's staff was starting to arrive. They all wore dark blue T-shirts with a special logo. Yet the animal handler was wearing a plaid shirt.

The door to Abby's office was partially open, and as he approached he felt a touch of cool air coming from inside. Preston stepped into the room, and Abby, who'd been sitting on the sofa next to the Navajo boy, came to meet him.

Now that he finally had a chance to take a closer, leisurely look at her, he realized that Abby Langdon was a stunner, with shoulder-length honey-brown hair and big hazel eyes. The loose clothing she wore didn't hide the fact that she had curves in all the right places.

"Did you figure out what happened?" Abby asked.

He shook his head. "It's much too soon for that, but I've got some more questions for you." Even as he spoke, he saw her expression turn from hopeful to disappointed. He softened his tone. "We'll get to the bottom of it, but these things take time. All I can tell you is that it wasn't an accident."

The color drained from her face. "This couldn't have had anything to do with our ranch. It has to be random...craziness."

"What do you know about the deceased?" he asked.

Her eyes widened. "You think Carl provoked this somehow? But that just can't be. He was a gentle man. He caught spiders and relocated rather than killed them."

"Relax. I'm just gathering information," he said.

She took a deep breath and nodded. "Sorry."

He saw her lips tremble but she quickly brought herself under control and turned her head to smile at Bobby.

Preston liked her. It was a purely instinctive reaction, but he trusted his gut. Just past those beautiful hazel eyes and that shaky smile beat the heart of a warrior. Yet hers was a gentle toughness.

The boy rose to his feet and came over. "I'm Bobby Neskahi," he said. Honoring Navajo ways, he didn't offer to shake hands. "I knew...him," he said, avoiding the name of the deceased, also according to Navajo custom. "Probably better than almost anyone," he added.

Preston wondered if the kid had been raised a traditionalist or was simply showing him the proper cultural respect.

"I'm *Diné*," Bobby said.

"We both are," Preston said, trying not to smile. *Diné* meant The People and signified those of the Navajo tribe.

Bobby moved back to the couch, and as he walked, Preston realized that the kid was no stranger to pain.

"Can we talk alone—Navajo to Navajo?" Bobby asked.

"Of course," Preston said, then looked at Abby.

"I'm not sure that's a good idea," she said, giving Preston a wary look.

"We'll keep it informal, not official." At her hesitation, he met her gaze. Looking someone in the eye was considered rude inside the Navajo Nation, but he'd learned over the years that those outside the tribe found it a sign of honesty, not disrespect. Though it hadn't come naturally to him, over time he'd adapted to the custom.

"Okay, but I'm staying right outside."

As Abby left, Preston sat down on the couch and gestured with a nod for Bobby to do the same. "Abby told me that you were the one who found the body this morning," Preston said.

He nodded and swallowed hard. "Yeah, but I stuck to the rule of three."

"I know," Preston said. "So tell me, Bobby, how well did you know the ranch's animal trainer?"

"Do you want me to avoid using his name or not?" Bobby asked. "I wasn't raised on the Rez but I don't want you to think I don't know any better."

"It's safe to use his name. I'm a police officer, so I'm a modernist."

"Mrs. Nez has been teaching me about our ways. She says modernists are like apples—red on the outside and white on the inside."

Preston laughed. It was an old saying, and he had a feeling Bobby was testing him. "I've heard it all, kid." He gazed into Bobby's hard brown eyes and for a moment saw a glimpse of himself at that age. He'd been so afraid to show vulnerability. The world was seldom kind to those perceived as weak. That was a lesson he'd learned in foster care quickly enough, and he had a feeling it was even more so for Bobby.

"Abby's trying to be brave, but on the inside she's scared. This isn't her fault, so you need to fix it."

"Fix it how?"

"Catch the bad guy before she freaks out. I can help. Carl and I were buds."

"Okay. Let's start at the beginning. First of all, what were you doing here so early in the morning?" Preston asked.

"I always come in super early because my foster father—

Mr. Jack is what we call him—drops me off on his way to work. He has his own janitorial company, and some of the places he cleans want everything done before they open for business."

"Okay, that answers that. So what do you usually do when you get here?"

"I say hi to Abby, then go help Carl feed the animals. He starts work even earlier than my foster dad."

"Tell me what you saw this morning," Preston pressed.

"I was going past the pens when I saw him just lying there on the ground. I saw the blood on his clothes and got scared so I went to get Abby." He paused, then looked up at Preston. "The horses weren't anywhere near him."

"Tell me more about Carl," Preston said.

"Carl was really old, like sixty. What I liked most about him was that he treated me just like he did everyone else," Bobby said, then looked away and wiped a tear from his face with a swipe of his hands. "He never gave me that 'poor kid' look. To him I was just me." He stared at his right leg, which was encased in a brace.

Bobby became quiet and Preston didn't interrupt the silence.

"Carl didn't have a lot of friends, kinda like me at the foster home." Bobby looked up at Preston and met his gaze. "He talked to the rest of the staff and all, but they weren't really his friends. He only had one other friend besides me and Abby. Rod Garner, Lightning Rod, who used to be in the NBA. Carl liked going over there and playing one-on-one with Lightning. Mr. Garner's got a huge basketball court—six goals. I've never been there, but Carl told me about it."

Preston nodded, beginning to understand Bobby more. "So what else did you two talk about?"

"Stuff," he said with a shrug. "We were always solving puzzles and riddles like real spies, you know? That was fun.

Carl liked games where you had to use your head, not your thumbs, and hated games where you had to trust your luck."

"You mean like gambling?"

"Yeah, like that. I tried to give him a buck once so he'd buy me a scratcher, but he wouldn't do it. I said I'd split the money if I won, but he still said no. Told me gambling was like throwing your money away and I was too smart to fall for stuff like that."

"He was telling you the truth. The odds always favor the game, not the gambler. Lottery, scratchers, casinos—they're all the same except for the odds."

"Don't you think that sometimes you just have to take a chance?" he said.

Preston didn't answer. "What would you have done with the money had you won?" he asked, trying to get a better handle on Bobby.

"Give it to Abby," he said without any hesitation. "She needs the money to keep the ranch and help kids like me. I wish she could find a rich guy to marry—someone who could help run the ranch and pay the bills. Do you know any rich guys?"

Preston heard coughing—more like choking—and Abby walked in a heartbeat later. From all indications, she'd been listening.

"Michelle's here, Bobby. She can give you a ride back home."

"Not now. Let me stay and help. You'll need to look in Carl's office, and if I go with you I can tell if anything's missing or been moved around."

Abby looked at Preston. "Bobby's got a photographic memory—really," she said.

"Not just that. I rule when it comes to puzzles and problem solving, too." He looked at Preston. "You don't believe me? Okay. I'll prove it." He gave Preston a once-over. "Betcha you spent some time outside working earlier this morning."

Preston smiled slowly. "How do you know that?"

"Your boots are real dusty but the dust is darker than the ground around here. You also have some red horse hair on you and we don't have any red horses. You were probably chopping wood or weeds or working real hard without gloves, 'cause the palms of your hands are all scuffed up. Maybe rope burns?" Bobby offered.

Preston smiled slowly. "Good observations. You might be another Sherlock Holmes someday, kid."

"Maybe. So can I stay?" he said, looking over at Abby. "Please?"

"Okay, but I need to speak to the detective alone right now. Go help Michelle feed the llamas."

"Sure." He turned to Preston. "We're counting on you, okay?" he said, then walked slowly out the door, closing it behind him. Abby waited several seconds before speaking. "I was eavesdropping because I didn't think it was a good idea for Bobby to speak to you alone. You don't know a thing about that boy."

"That was the purpose of talking to him."

"I still think you should have had an adult present."

"He found the body, but he's not a suspect," Preston said. "You seem to have heard pretty much everything we talked about, so why are you worried?"

"You don't understand. Bobby sometimes comes across as a tough kid and in a lot of ways he is, but he's been betrayed and abandoned by people all his life. Carl was one of the few adults he trusted. Now he's gone, too. Can you imagine what he's going through? You have to cut him some slack and be careful what kind of questions you ask him. It's important that he continue to remember Carl in a good way."

What touched Preston most was her protectiveness. When

he'd been Bobby's age, he, too, would have gone to the wall for anyone who'd cared enough to defend him.

"I have no intention of doing anything that would hurt Bobby. I'll be careful around him, but I'm here to do a job. That means digging for the truth even if it turns out to be something you don't want to hear."

"All right. The truth doesn't frighten me. How can I help you find answers?"

"Let's start with some straight talk."

Chapter Four

Abby watched Detective Bowman as he checked his notes. He was handsome in a tough, streetwise way. Somewhere along the way he'd shrugged out of his police-issue jacket and was now wearing a navy shirt with the sleeves rolled up.

He looked muscular, like a man used to hard, physical work. His shoulders were wide, and his chest was as broad and strong as she remembered from this morning. She suppressed a sigh. He wasn't a pretty boy. His nose was a little crooked, like he'd broken it at one time, but that just heightened his appeal.

Detective Preston Bowman was fascinating to watch. Even as he wrote in his notebook she could sense a restless energy about him.

As he shifted, her gaze fell to the badge clipped to his belt and, on the other side, his handgun. That reminder was all she needed to rein in her thoughts. He was a law enforcement professional here to do a job, and this was no time for distractions.

"Carl didn't have a vehicle, so I'm assuming he had a bicycle or drove one of the ranch's trucks?" he asked.

As he looked at her, she felt the power of his gaze all through her. Detective Bowman was all male, with cool eyes that didn't miss much and left her feeling slightly off balance.

"What is that, Detective—a trick question? You've undoubtedly already run his name through the MVD and know that Carl didn't have a driver's license. If he needed to go someplace, he either hitched a ride with one of our volunteers or rode his bicycle, which is in his office in the barn."

Preston held her gaze a moment longer, but she forced herself not to even blink.

"You paid him by check?"

"Yeah, but he preferred cash. He didn't have a bank account," she said.

He looked at her, surprised. "And that didn't seem odd to you?"

"Carl was one of a kind," she said with a sad smile. "He also didn't have a credit card or a cell phone. In this day and age, that's hard to believe, but it's true."

"No prepaid cell phone either?"

"I can't say for sure, but I really doubt it. It just wasn't his style." As much as she wanted to trust him, she knew they weren't really on the same side. He was here only to investigate the crime. Her priority was protecting the ranch and, more importantly, the work they did here.

"After we're done and the scene is released, do you plan to reopen right away?"

"I haven't decided yet," she said, then as her voice wavered, she swallowed hard. "Without knowing why someone came after me, I can't guarantee anyone's safety. Just being around me could endanger the kids and I can't let that happen."

"I can't give you any real assurances, but based on the evidence, the guy who jumped you didn't want you dead. He had his chance. My guess is that he only wanted to scare you."

"Do you think it was the same person who killed Carl?"

"Not likely. Woods died last night, between nine and midnight approximately. That means his killer would have had to stick around for six to nine hours."

"But *two* violent incidents that close together? That's a huge coincidence, don't you think? We've never had any trouble here," she said. "Let's assume the killer did stick around. What do you think he did all that time?"

"Searching for something? You tell me. This is your ranch, so your guess will probably be better than mine."

Hearing a knock on the door, she excused herself and went to answer it. A tall, wiry, redheaded man in a Western shirt and jeans came in.

"Stan," she said.

The man took her hand for a moment. "Abby, I'm so sorry. Carl was a good man."

She gestured toward Preston. "This is Detective Bowman from the Hartley police," she said. "He's investigating Carl's death." The words sounded odd even in her own ears. "Detective, this is Stan Cooper, my accountant and business advisor."

"You can add ranch volunteer to that list, too," he said, brushing alfalfa leaves off his shirt instead of offering to shake hands. "I just brought in a trailer loaded with hay, saw the police and learned what happened."

"I'm still trying to come to terms with everything," Abby said.

"I know this is hard on you, Abby, but you've got a more immediate problem. Some kids with special needs have just arrived, and right behind them is a camera crew from the local cable TV station."

She rubbed her forehead with her fingertips and closed her eyes for a second, trying to push back a migraine. "I made a lot of calls already this morning, but I couldn't reach everyone, particularly the ones who were already on their way."

"That's okay. Put it out of your mind. Right now you're going to have to go out there and make a statement to the press," Stan said. "You need to make sure everyone understands that the ranch will have to remain closed for the time being. Explain that your priority is cooperating with the police so this unfortunate incident can be cleared up. Don't let them draw you into long discussions. Keep it short and simple."

She nodded. "I'll handle it."

"After the initial interview, don't talk to the press again," Stan said. "Stay low profile. That's my professional and personal advice. The longer this story remains front-page news, the worse off the ranch will be. Something like this could scare away current and future benefactors."

Abby moved to the window and looked outside. "I really don't want to turn those kids away now that they're here. They really look forward to spending time at the ranch and I hate disappointing them."

Preston followed her gaze. "Is it just those three kids?"

"Yes. I got hold of the others due in today and told them I'd reschedule."

"If you could keep them well away from the crime scene area, you could still let them ride the horses and pet the other animals," Preston said.

"Absolutely not," Stan said quickly. "Abby, think about it. The media is already out there taking photos. If you say that the ranch will have to be closed for now, people will see that as your way of putting the kids' safety first. Yet if you say that's what you're going to do and then invite those kids in, you'll lose credibility. The public will see images of kids riding horses and petting camels right next to half a dozen police cars and lots of yellow crime scene tape. Your donors are going to run for cover."

"I'll figure this out, Stan. Stop worrying," Abby said firmly.

As she stepped out of the office, she had no idea what she was going to say. Then, making a spur-of-the-moment decision, Abby went to meet the kids. After briefly explaining the situation to the adults who'd brought them, she focused on the children.

"I know you've all been looking forward to this, but the police have important work they need to finish." Abby glanced at Lilly, a small seven-year-old girl who'd been to the ranch once before. Her illness was terminal and, with her, each day counted. The other two, both boys, were new to Standing Tall Ranch.

"So we have to go back?" Lilly asked, her expression so downcast it tugged at Abby.

"I'll tell you what. There can be no horseback riding this time, but how would you like to come say hello to Hank and Eli, our camels?" She saw their faces brighten.

"I'm Jason," the tallest boy said, balancing well on two prosthetic legs. "I'm eight and I've never even seen a camel. Can we pet them?"

"I'd like that too," the other boy said. "I'm Carlos."

Abby recognized him from his file. Carlos was a victim of abuse and still had trust issues.

"Are they friendly?" Carlos added.

"Absolutely. We'll pick up some treats for them as we go over to their pens."

Out of the corner of her eye, Abby saw a camera crew hurrying over to her, but the detective moved quickly to intercept them.

A wave of relief swept over her and she smiled. She liked that man already. Beneath the stern cop exterior was a gentle heart. She'd make sure to thank him later.

PRESTON IDENTIFIED HIMSELF to the reporters. He knew a few already, like Marsha Robertson. She was an area reporter for the number one network affiliate in the state, which was based in Albuquerque.

He gave them all a quick rundown. "That's all I have for you at this time."

"A source tells me the owner was also attacked," Marsha

said, "perhaps by the killer. How can you be sure that those kids are safe?"

"There are a dozen or more police officers here. They're safe, just as you are."

"Right now, sure, but later…then what? Once the crime scene is released and the officers all leave, will Sitting Tall Ranch open up and return to business as usual?"

"That's a question you'll have to ask the owner."

"And that would be me," Abby said, walking up with Bobby at her side.

"The safety of the children always comes first, so the ranch will be closed until we can find out exactly what happened. I've made an exception for those kids because they were already here. Our riding instructor, Michelle Okerman, will stay with them while I speak to you, and if you'll glance over from time to time, you'll see the difference just being around the animals makes to these children."

Abby paused and looked directly at each reporter there. "This ranch is a nonprofit whose sole purpose is to brighten the lives of kids who might otherwise have very little to smile about. One of our guests today is in the last stages of a serious illness and deserves extra consideration. That's why I decided to let Sitting Tall Ranch rise above its present circumstances and come through on promises made."

Preston saw that Abby's answer had hit just the right tone with the reporters. He had a feeling more donations would soon come in. In fact, he intended to send her a check himself.

As the reporters moved away, Stan approached and said, "Well played."

"I didn't *play,* Stan. I told them the truth."

"Yes, well, now concentrate on staying low profile till this blows over."

"And that'll be soon, right?" Bobby asked, looking up at

Preston. "The CSI unit will get DNA from something, or trace evidence, and then you'll go arrest the bad guy."

"I wish it were that simple, but it's not. Right now we're gathering evidence, and then we'll be interviewing a lot of people. Once we have a suspect, we'll move in and arrest him or her." Seeing Officer Michaels signal him, Preston excused himself momentarily.

"What's up?" he asked Michaels as he walked over to the barn.

"We processed, photographed and logged in the evidence. When will you be ready for us to process the vic's residence, the bunkhouse?"

"Hang on. I want a chance to look around there first. Did you or Gabe interview the staff?"

"Everyone who's on-site now, yes. That includes the riding instructor, Michelle Okerman. She teaches the kids about balance and paying attention. Basically, she walks next to the mounts and helps them each step of the way. Monroe Jenkins, the police chief's son, is here this morning, too. He volunteers a lot in the summer and does whatever needs to be done. Ilse Sheridan is also here. She's Lightning Rod Garner's personal assistant and volunteers her time to help train the horses. The last time any of them claim to have seen the vic was yesterday afternoon."

"Thanks. I'll let you know when you can process the bunkhouse. In the meantime, walk through the grounds and check out each of the other structures. We don't know where else the intruder went. And verify that there's a bicycle inside the barn office."

Michaels nodded. "Got it. We've already set up a search pattern."

When Preston returned to where Abby was standing, Bobby was speaking to Michelle. The boy was favoring his right leg and swaying slightly from side to side.

Abby followed his line of vision. "He's conning her," she whispered with a tiny smile. "Michelle was hoping to divert Bobby by asking him to talk to the kids, but he knows where the action's going to be. He'd rather stick with us."

"That kid's in pain. I don't think he's faking it," Preston said.

"His disability is real, but he's learned to use it. Don't ever underestimate him. Bobby's highly intelligent and knows how to manipulate adults to get out of whatever he doesn't want to do."

Preston didn't comment, still unconvinced.

"Jack Yarrow, his foster parent, prefers dropping him off here first thing in the morning because Bobby makes his wife nervous. He can read her like a book and tells her what she's about to do next, which creeps her out big-time."

"He's incredibly observant," he said with a smile.

"It's all part of a game he plays. Bobby can't let go of the hope that he and his biological father will be together again someday. After his dad gave him up, Bobby made up the story that his dad's in the CIA and had to leave to protect him. He told it so many times, he actually began to believe it. He reads everything he can about spy craft and pretends he's training so he can join his dad someday."

"He's protecting himself from a truth that hurts too much to accept," Preston said, remembering his days in foster care.

"The problem is that this game he plays often gets him into trouble. When he's told not to do something, he pretends he's a spy on a secret mission and finds a way to do it anyway," she said. "I'm willing to bet that most of the time he doesn't get caught."

"He may be a handful, but he's got a lot going for him," Preston said, chuckling. "Kids who've been bounced around often need something or someone to believe in. Bobby had a hard time finding that, so he created it. In my mind that deserves a high five."

Just then Bobby came up. "When will you be checking out Carl's office?"

"I'm going over to the bunkhouse now," Preston said. "I'll check the office after that."

"Great. I can help you at both places. I've been at the bunkhouse lots of times too," he said.

Abby gave him a surprised look. "You have?"

"Sure, after Carl finished his chores, he and I would play games. We both loved anagrams and riddles, and sometimes we'd make up our own codes and send each other secret messages."

"On a computer?" Preston asked.

"No," Bobby said. "Just on paper. He was *good,* too. We'd try to make the codes impossible to break, like real spies would, but he'd win most of the time."

"What happened when you won?" Preston asked, following his gut.

Bobby smiled. "I'd get to feed the camels."

"Alone?" Abby asked, her voice rising.

"No, Carl would always stay with me, watching, but I'd be the one who did it," he said, a touch of pride in his voice.

"Sounds like the camels are your favorites," Preston said.

"Yeah, Hank and Eli are cool. They remember stuff. There's one guy who swatted Eli just to get him out of the way once, and Eli never forgot. After that, he'd set the guy up by acting real calm, then biting at him the second he got close."

"Are you talking about Joe Brown?" Abby asked.

Bobby nodded.

"I caught him manhandling one of the horses and fired him on the spot," she told Preston.

"I'm going to need to interview everyone who might have had some grievance against the victim or the ranch. Can you get me a list of all current and past employees, say, going back six months?" Preston said.

"No problem," Abby said.

As they headed toward the bunkhouse, Bobby slipped in smoothly between Preston and Abby. Preston noted it silently, wondering if the boy had a crush on Abby. Or maybe there was more at play. Considering Bobby's past, it was possible the kid didn't trust cops.

"So Carl had the use of the bunkhouse rent free?" Preston verified as they neared the small building about the size of a one-car garage or a startup home on the Rez.

"It was part of the package since I couldn't pay him what he was worth. Carl agreed to fix up the interior for me, too, as long as I purchased the supplies," she said. "When I first bought Sitting Tall Ranch, the property had been unoccupied for years. Everything had been neglected and most of the buildings were practically unlivable."

He looked around. The barn and storage sheds had fresh coats of paint, the corrals had up-to-date welded pipe fencing and the areas were well maintained. There wasn't a weed in sight.

"You've done a good job. The place shows the care you give it."

"That's what you do with a dream," she said softly, then unlocked the bunkhouse door.

Chapter Five

Preston put on a fresh pair of gloves as he stepped inside. "Come in with me, but *don't* touch anything," he told them. "And be careful where you step. If there's something on the floor, leave it there."

Preston remained in the doorway a few seconds longer and just looked around. He'd expected a utilitarian place designed to fit the needs of its one resident, and he'd been right on target. The interior held the stamp of the working man who'd lived here.

An easy chair made of blue vinyl and patched with duct tape in several places was backed against one wall. A small table a few feet in front of it held an old TV with rabbit ears and the digital converter box needed to translate the signal.

There were pencil and black ink sketches on the wall and the supplies needed for more—stiff white paper, charcoal sticks, markers and pencils—on the shelf of a nearby empty bookcase.

"He loved to draw," Bobby said, standing at the doorway with Preston, "but he threw out most of his stuff. If he wasn't happy with the way it came out, it went straight into the trash."

Abby nodded. "I tried to salvage a charcoal sketch he'd thrown out once, but he wouldn't let me keep it. When I gave it back to him, he just tore it up. He made me another one, though, and I hung it in the main house, my home."

Preston led the way into the room, then saw Bobby staring at the bookshelf. "Something missing?" he asked the boy.

"Yeah, his coffee can is gone," Bobby said.

"He kept coffee on the bookshelf?" Preston looked around for a coffeemaker but didn't see one.

"He drank coffee like crazy, but it was all instant," Bobby said. "The coffee can was his bank—that's what he called it. It was old, like from twenty years ago, and all dented. He said that he used to buy that brand when he was a lot younger and having it around brought back good memories." Bobby paused, swallowed hard, then in a heavy voice added, "He told me about it being his bank because we were friends and he trusted me."

Abby stepped closer to Bobby and said, "How about we wait outside for you, Detective?"

Bobby shook his head. "No, I'm okay. I just miss him, that's all. Let me stay and help."

Preston heard Abby sigh and saw her nod.

"Anything else that looks out of place, Bobby? Walk around and take a good look, but remember, don't touch anything," Preston said.

Abby stayed right beside Bobby as they took the lead. Preston followed, his gaze on Abby. She was leggy and had a great figure, but what appealed to him most had little to do with her looks.

She was obviously a woman whose feelings ran deep. She cared a lot for Bobby and the rest of the kids who came to the ranch. He made a mental note to find out more about her, and not just because she was part of the case he was working.

They passed through a narrow hall and an open door and entered Carl's bedroom. Inside they found an unmade bed, one wooden chair, an old oak desk and a small three-drawer chest. On top of the desk were several lottery tickets, two scratchers, tickets from a slot machine and a couple of chips from the casino.

"You sure he didn't gamble?" Preston asked Bobby.

"I never saw stuff like that here before. There's no way those were his. He thought gambling was stupid. Someone must have put them there," Bobby said. Then he pointed to the coffee can on top of the chest of drawers. "He didn't keep the can there either. It was always out front, on that shelf."

Preston lifted the lid, but there was no cash inside, only two more lottery tickets.

"Think hard, Bobby. Did you ever see the cash that was supposedly inside the can?"

"I never looked inside it—that would have been rude. But he wouldn't have lied to me," Bobby said.

Abby smiled at Bobby, then looked at Preston. "I can tell you this much—Carl was always careful with his money. He had to be. He never wasted a dollar."

"Yeah, Detective Bowman," Bobby said. "I'm just a kid, but I know serious gamblers. That's all they talk about—winning, betting, the odds."

"Did you learn that from your parents?" Preston asked.

"No, no way. My mom died when I was three or four, and my dad, well, he gave me up 'cause he's a spy and can't afford to have a kid hanging around. He travels all over the world," Bobby said proudly. "I know about gamblers because my last foster dad had the habit. All those guys ever talk about is hitting the big time."

"Carl wouldn't even take part in the dollar World Series pool or the weekly football winners the staff had," Abby said.

"And why would anyone keep losing tickets?" Bobby said, pointing to the desk. "People throw that stuff out once they find out they lost." He paused, then added quickly, "They *are* losing tickets, right?"

Preston glanced down. "I'll have to check the numbers, but

the scratchers are no good." He entered the numbers into his notebook, then put it into his pocket.

"You need to get your lab guys in here and fingerprint this entire place! Like on TV. Especially those tickets. Once you find who put them there, you'll be able to close the case. Right?" Bobby asked, his voice rising with excitement.

"We'll need more than that, Bobby, but we'll start by taking prints," Preston said. "There's a uniformed officer outside named Michaels. Can you find him for me?"

"Sure!" Bobby turned around, lost his balance for a second and fell against Preston.

Preston helped steady him.

"Let go. I'm fine," Bobby muttered.

As Bobby ambled off in a rush to go, his side-to-side gait was barely noticeable.

Preston took a step and instantly noticed that his jacket pocket felt lighter. It didn't take him long to put things together. Bobby hadn't accidentally lost his balance at all. He'd had a specific goal in mind.

Preston nearly laughed out loud. He wouldn't say anything right now, but he'd settle this with the kid later.

"Did you see that? Bobby left with scarcely a trace of a limp," Abby said. "When he's excited or distracted, he isn't so aware of the things that are wrong with his body. I first noticed that when my twin sister got sick, and that's what eventually led me to open Sitting Tall Ranch. Here kids have something fun to do and think about. We lift their spirits and, believe it or not, that's a big part of the battle."

"What happened to your sister?" he asked.

She shook her head and looked away, her eyes misty. "Another time."

Sensing that she regretted having spoken so freely, he dropped it for now. "I haven't seen any mail around here anywhere," he said, focusing back on work. "Did Carl have a post office box?"

"Not that I know of," Abby said.

"No bank account, no bills… Something's not right," he said, thinking out loud.

"I paid his utility bills," she said. "I know it sounds like a really sweet deal, but Carl could have worked at any ranch in the county for far more than what I could pay him. He was the best animal trainer I've ever seen."

"Exactly what kind of training did he do for you?"

"He made sure the horses were worked daily and that they'd respond to cues without any problems. He also worked with the llamas and made sure they'd be steady and reliable around the kids. We also use the camels for promos and fundraisers. Hank, in particular, can be terribly stubborn, and if he gets mad, he'll just refuse to cooperate. Away from the ranch that can be a problem, but when Carl went along, they were always on their best behavior."

As Officer Michaels came into the bunkhouse, Preston went to meet him. "Have the team process this place and collect fingerprints. I have reason to suspect the killer was here."

"Got it. And in answer to the bike question, there's an old five-speed in the barn office."

"Thanks," Preston said, then looked over at Abby.

"That's Carl's," she confirmed.

After Michaels left, Preston placed the casino tickets and other gambling pieces in an evidence bag, then signed and dated it. "I'll follow up on this personally."

"Can you let me know what you find out?" Abby asked.

"Not right away. This is a police matter now, but I will say this—I have a reputation for closing my cases. I never give up till the job's done."

"We have that in common."

"You built this place from scratch. Is that right?"

"Yeah, and it didn't happen overnight. The only reason I succeeded was because I refused to take my eyes off the goal."

"That's the way I work, too."

"So what's next?"

"I'll go through this place with the crime scene team. I find it hard to believe the victim was so out of touch with modern-day society—no phone, no bank account and so on. My gut tells me that he was hiding something. Maybe we'll find some answers here in the bunkhouse."

As the crime scene team moved in, Preston met them at the door. "Keep a lookout for any paper trail—mail, bills, receipts, social, anything. There's got to be more to this guy than we've seen so far."

Preston remained with the crime scene unit and worked alongside them for another hour. After finding nothing, he went back to the ranch's office. The hopeful look on Abby's face speared through him.

"Did you find something helpful?" she asked.

"No. I'm sorry. Sometimes progress on a case doesn't come quickly or easily."

"I'd never say this in front of Bobby, but I'm terrified the man who killed Carl will come back for me," she whispered, standing by the window and watching Bobby speak to the kids. "Is it safe for any of us here now?"

He wanted to hold her like he'd done before and calm her, but the badge at his belt kept him where he was. "Miss Langdon, we'll have patrol officers close by tonight," he said, using a professional tone of voice, something experience told him would give her the added confidence she needed. "If there's any problem at all, dial 911. You'll have help almost immediately."

"Thank you," she said then with a shaky smile, added, "And call me Abby, please. You saved my life."

"Abby it is then," he said. "Call me Preston."

"Preston," she repeated, as if savoring the name.

Calling her by her first name made good sense. He had to establish rapport with a witness and victim. But deep down he knew his motives weren't strictly aboveboard and professional.

He liked Abby and that could be a problem. He wouldn't have given a strictly physical attraction a second thought—one night or two of hot sex, then move on. But he wanted to be personally involved this time—to help her even the odds and to protect her as if she belonged to him somehow. Maybe it had something to do with how she'd felt in his arms—her scent.

Trouble. That's all that could come of this. Enough.

Before he could say anything else there was a knock on the semi-opened door. It was Gabe Sanchez, an officer from the crime scene unit.

"We're wrapping up here for now," he said. "Anything else you need from me?"

"Process the prints as soon as you can," Preston said, going to meet him. "I'll be heading to the casino next to follow up on those receipts and chips."

"Without a warrant? Better come on strong, put your bad cop on and hope it's enough."

"We'll see how far I get," he said with a shrug.

After Gabe left, Preston went back into the room where Abby waited.

"I gather you're expecting trouble with the casino staff. If you are, maybe I can help."

"What's your connection with that place?"

"Lightning Rod Garner, the former NBA star, is one of the ranch's biggest supporters. He's also one of the casino's main shareholders. Do you know him?"

"Only by reputation. He's had a few run-ins with the police," Preston said with a scowl. "Temper, mostly."

She smiled hesitantly. "I know he can be hard to deal with, particularly if he doesn't consider you a friend, but deep down, he's a good man. Let me take you over and introduce you. That should help."

"I'll keep your offer in mind, but right now I'd like you to check your files and give me the name of Carl's next of kin."

It had been no more than a flash in her eyes, but his link to Falcon helped him see what was necessary. More attuned to Abby now, he sensed worry and nervousness—classic signs that she was holding something back.

"If he had any relatives, he never spoke about them, nor did he list them in his employment application." Then, in a gentle voice, she added, "He was a solitary man but not an unhappy one. He enjoyed his job and life here at the ranch."

Falcon's gaze didn't miss much. Abby was hiding something from him, and one way or another he was going to find out what that was.

"Carl Woods seems to be surrounded by mystery, but it won't stay that way for long. No matter how deeply buried, secrets are never safe from me."

Her eyes widened and as he held her gaze, he saw the unmistakable glimmer of fear.

Chapter Six

Abby handed Carl's employee file to Preston. "That's all the information I have."

Before he could comment, Bobby came in. "My foster mom's here. I have a doctor's appointment this afternoon. I'll be back just as soon as I can, okay?"

"No, Bobby, stay at home until I call you," Abby said. "We have to keep the ranch closed for now. It may not be safe for you here."

"But—" Bobby stopped speaking abruptly, looked at the floor, then back up at her. "Can I talk to you for just a minute—alone?" he added.

Leaving Preston behind, Abby met with Bobby in the kitchen area. "Okay, what's up?"

"You haven't been around cops much, Abby, and I want you to know that you can't always trust them. They might pretend to be your friend, but they're not."

"You think Detective Bowman is like that?"

"Probably. When one of the kids at the foster home is hassled by the cops, the officers always come to talk to the rest of us. They try to trick us into telling them stuff so they can put the one they're after in jail."

"Maybe the problem isn't the cops but what the kids did to get the attention of the police."

"Abby, you're a good person, but don't trust him. He thinks you're keeping secrets from him."

"What makes you say that?" she asked quickly.

A horn blared outside. "Mrs. Yarrow doesn't like waiting. I better go."

Abby watched Bobby hurry to the door, but before he could step outside, Preston stopped him.

"Before you leave, Bobby, how about giving me back my notebook?"

Bobby smiled. "Hey, yeah. You dropped it back at Carl's place. Guess I forgot to give it back."

Abby watched the exchange. "He picked your pocket, didn't he?" she asked as soon as Bobby was gone.

Preston smiled but didn't answer.

"Don't be angry with him. I know it was wrong, but he was trying to protect me. In his experience, cops haven't always been the good guys," she said. "He's afraid you might hurt me or the ranch and probably wanted to slow you down."

"He's a great little pickpocket—I'll give him that," Preston said. "It took me a couple of seconds to notice what he'd done."

"Are you going to press charges?"

"Nah, I got it back, and I can't fault him for wanting to protect a friend."

"He doesn't have many of those. There's not a lot of common ground between him and the other boys at the foster home, so they tend to give him a hard time."

"Kids often target anyone who's different from them," Preston said. "That can be especially bad at a foster home because you're in such close quarters."

"You've dealt with kids from foster homes before?"

"You might say that—I was one," he said.

"You grew up in foster care?" she asked.

"Yeah. I had a tough time of it until *Hosteen* Silver, a medicine man from our tribe, decided to foster me. I met my five brothers there at his home," he said and smiled, remembering. "It took time for us to become a family, but we're all close now."

"Bobby would love a chance like that. He wants to know about his tribe, but the only real contact he has is the cook at the foster home, Mrs. Nez."

"*Hosteen* Silver was a remarkable man. He gave my brothers and me the confidence we needed to leave the past behind us and take charge of our lives."

"The kids who come here are all facing tough times. They're not in charge of anything—not their bodies or their lives. Helping them forget their troubles for a while strengthens them so they can continue their fight."

He paused for a moment. "You love this ranch and are committed to the work you do. I get that," he said at last, "but by holding back you're not helping anyone, least of all yourself."

Before she could answer, Michelle came rushing in. "We've got a problem. Stan was helping out by cleaning the camels' pen but somehow he ended up in the corner. Now every time he tries to go past Hank, the animal threatens to bite him."

"I better get over there. Without Carl, this falls to me," she told Preston. "I think Hank must have misinterpreted something Stan did. Camels are practically famous for holding grudges."

"I'll go with you. Maybe I can help," he said.

They reached the large enclosure a few minutes later. Stan was against the fence opposite the gate wiping a green wet mixture off his shirt. "Hank's in a bad, bad mood today. He spit at me."

"Actually, they don't spit. They throw up on you." She gave him a sheepish smile. "That doesn't help much, does it?"

"No," Stan said, scowling. "Now I'm grossed out."

"We'll get you out, then Michelle and I will finish up here," Abby said, then glanced back at Preston. She was going to explain to him that Hank loved women and children, but when she turned, she saw Hank nuzzling Preston like an old friend.

Her mouth fell open.

Stan stared. "How did you do that?" he asked, quickly moving out of the pen.

"It goes back to something my foster father taught me," Preston said calmly. "All things—including animals and people—are connected. I approached the camel enclosure with a Song of Blessing, what we call a *Hozonji*. I honored the link between us and the camel responded by doing the same. It's all about showing respect and demanding the same in return."

Abby wondered if he was trying to send her a message. Was he telling her to respect his profession and trust him to solve the case? His eyes held hers with an intensity that left her feeling bare…and exposed somehow.

Hank stretched his rubbery lips, trying to kiss Preston.

Abby laughed. "They're really gentle creatures. They're calmer than horses but they're more…emotional," she said after a beat. "How would you feel about volunteering here sometime?"

"After the case is closed, I'll do my best to fit some hours into my schedule."

"Good."

Preston glanced at his watch. "I need to go now and check out a few things. Make sure no one goes into the areas that are cordoned off."

"All right. Do you know how long it'll be before the yellow tape can be taken down?"

"I'm not sure. Some details need to be handled first. I'll let you know as soon as possible."

Abby walked back to the parking lot with him. "Carl's killer took the life of a very good man. He's done enough damage. Don't let him harm my ranch, too. Find answers quickly, Preston, please."

"We want the same thing, but you're holding out on me, Abby, and that's slowing me down. Eventually, I'll uncover whatever it is you're keeping back. Save us both some time and come clean."

He stopped walking and looked directly at her without so much as a blink. She shifted uncomfortably. There was an intensity about Preston that left her feeling off balance. She wasn't in control—he was. The message was clear.

"I know nothing that can help you find the killer," she said.

"Let me be the judge."

She stared at the ground. Maybe he did deserve to know, but some secrets weren't hers to tell. Finally looking up, she shook her head.

"If you want me to catch the killer quickly, Abby, don't stand in my way."

Before she could answer, he strode away from her with the long, confident steps of a man used to being in charge.

She watched him for a moment longer. He was all steady strength and power kept in reserve. For a second her thoughts drifted and she wondered what it would be like to lay in his arms, to touch and caress him until passion overcame all reason. It was the man beyond that iron will, the one hidden by the badge, who she wanted to see most of all.

Realizing the turn of her thoughts, she sighed. She was truly losing her mind.

Glancing around, she forced her thoughts back on the ranch. She couldn't do anything more for Carl, but the ranch needed her now. Seeing Stan and Michelle outside the barn pointing up at the weathered roof, she knew what had to be done next.

Making an impromptu decision, she headed to her truck. Maybe she couldn't help Preston catch Carl's killer, but she knew how to raise badly needed cash. Her first order of business—pay Rod Garner a visit.

Chapter Seven

As Preston drove west in the direction of the casino, he thought about Abby's offer to talk to Garner. If he hadn't been the kind who went by the book, he might have taken her up on it. The casino visit was bound to be a train wreck. He and Jennifer Graham, the head of security there, had a history. They'd dated for a while, and things hadn't ended well. She'd wanted more—he'd wanted less.

Maybe he *was* going in the wrong direction. He pulled off the road, waited for a break in traffic, then turned around. All things considered, he might be better off talking to Rod Garner first. Garner and Carl had supposedly been friends, so that gave him some leverage. With a little luck, Garner would help the investigation along by giving him fresh insights into the victim.

If things went smoothly, he'd also try to persuade Garner to pull some strings for him at the casino. He had to convince Jennifer to give the department access to surveillance videos. Verifying that Carl had been there on certain dates and finding out who he'd come into contact with might help establish a motive and suggest a suspect. Of course, it was all speculation at this point, and he sure as heck didn't have enough for a court order.

He was headed to Garner's estate when his cell phone rang.

"I need your report, Sergeant," Preston heard Police Chief

Jenkins say as soon as he answered. "Miss Langdon and Sitting Tall Ranch are important to our community. They've put us on the map in a very good way. My own son works there as a volunteer."

Preston updated him on what he had so far. "I'm en route to Rod Garner's residence, sir. Garner was one of Carl Woods's friends, apparently."

"Interesting—a ranch hand and a millionaire former NBA star."

"Not what you'd expect, sir, but I've learned that Garner is also one of the ranch's benefactors. I think he'll cooperate with the investigation."

"Getting him on our side makes sense, Bowman. Garner's got a lot of fans, and if he gets the word out that he wants this resolved, we might get the cooperation of people who wouldn't ordinarily come within a mile of a cop."

"Yeah, that's my take, too. Unfortunately Garner also has a reputation as a troublemaker, so I'll have to tread carefully."

"Whatever it takes. Keep me updated," the chief said, then ended the call.

As Preston pulled into the long, tree-lined driveway of the former basketball star's home, he saw a familiar pickup at the far end. Sitting Tall's logo was emblazoned on one of the doors.

Reaching the parking area, Preston glanced around and saw Abby heading down the cobblestone walk toward the front entrance.

He parked beside her pickup and called out to her.

Abby turned her head, smiled and walked back to meet him.

"We must have just missed each other on the highway. I didn't expect to run into you here," he said, glad to see her anyway.

"I'm here to ask for a donation. We need a new roof on

the barn. There's no way it'll withstand the gusts and down-pours we get during monsoon season," she said. "Rod's always helped us when we're in a bind, and I'm hoping he'll come through for us again."

"Do you deal with him directly or talk to his assistant, Ilse Sheridan?"

"I speak to Rod. He trusts me and he likes being involved with the ranch. He believes in my dream."

"It's not a dream anymore," Preston said. "It's a reality."

"Some of it is, but there's so much more I'd like to do," she said, falling into step beside him. "I'd love to build special quarters that could accommodate a few overnight guests. A day at the ranch can really tire out some of the kids, and transportation can be an issue. If they could spend the night…"

Although she was still speaking, Preston's attention was momentarily diverted by two vehicles coming up the drive. The first was a small pickup with a dented fender. The bed of the truck was filled with gardening supplies. The driver, wearing a ball cap low on his head, pulled up and parked across the parking lot opposite to where they were standing.

As the driver climbed out, Preston noted that the floor of the cab was littered with beer bottles. If that was one of the estate's landscape people, Garner needed to take a closer look at the help.

The second vehicle, a long white limo, entered the lot and soon came to a stop in front of the walk. Like everyone else in town, Preston recognized Lightning Rod Garner's ride. Garner, who'd lost his license after his third DWI, had hired a local man as his full-time chauffeur. That level of luxury was almost unheard of in this part of the state except for weddings, funerals and homecoming dances.

As the limo driver came around to open the door for Garner, the man from the pickup quickened his pace and headed toward the big car. His stride was unsteady, like a man who'd had one too many, and he seemed oblivious to everything except Garner.

Preston caught a glimpse of what the man was holding just inside the sleeve of his jacket.

"Abby, move behind the engine block of your car *now*."

"What—"

"Do it."

As Preston moved to intercept the guy in the cap, the man's focus remained on Garner, who was just stepping out of the car.

Preston took advantage of the situation and moved forward quickly, drawing his weapon. Once he was within ten feet, the man finally turned his head and spotted him.

"Police officer! Put down the gun and lay flat on the ground. Now!"

The man swung his weapon around. Preston could have taken the shot at point-blank range but instead chopped down hard using his own pistol. He caught the man's wrist and knocked the gun out of his hand.

The guy yelped, then lunged for Preston's weapon.

Preston's hard left jab caught the guy in the jaw and the suspect staggered sideways and fell.

Preston moved in, forcing the suspect's face down into the gravel, then cuffed him.

"What the hell's going on?" Garner asked, rushing over.

"Stay back and call 911," Preston said.

AFTER TWO PATROL officers arrived to transport the assailant to the police station, Abby, Preston and Garner met in his home office. The wood-paneled room was huge and well appointed, and Preston took it all in slowly, thinking the house at Copper Canyon would probably fit in this space. Even the high ceiling, which incorporated a domed skylight, was composed of thick wooden beams and rich wood panels. The only place he'd ever seen an office like this was on TV.

Preston took a seat on a huge black leather sofa, and a leggy short-haired blonde wearing an expensive-looking tailored tan pantsuit appeared out of thin air and offered him a scotch.

"No, thanks. I'm on duty."

"I'll take one, Ilse. Bring me that special bottle I've been saving," Rod said. He looked at Preston. "Don't mind me, but I usually don't have people trying to gun me down. Wanting to kick my butt, yeah, but coming after me with a gun, no."

"Did you recognize the man who came for you?" Preston asked, watching out of the corner of his eye as the attractive blonde poured the scotch.

"Never seen him that I can recall," Rod said, taking the scotch and downing it with one swallow.

"His name is Phil Gorman. Does that ring a bell?"

Garner looked down at his empty glass as he shook his head. "Ilse, look up the name and see if he's ever done any work here."

"So you've never had any personal dealings with Gorman?" Preston insisted.

"Hey, dude, I see and talk to a lot of people, but I don't always remember them. Maybe I've seen him, maybe not, but he's no one I deal with regularly. That kind of contact I remember."

"Okay, fair enough," Preston said.

"Did he say why he came after me?" Rod leaned back on the plush leather chair and stretched out his legs. It was an action that made him seem even taller than his six-foot-eight frame and required a lot of room, which fortunately he had.

"Yeah. He blames you and the casino for his business troubles. I don't have details yet," Preston said.

"Another guy who can't man up and take responsibility

for himself. They're always looking for someone to blame," Rod muttered.

"I'm not so sure he's telling us the real story. I think there may be a lot more to the hit," Preston said. "First, Carl's murdered, then someone goes after Abby, now this."

"Someone attacked you?" Rod sat up and looked at Abby quickly. "You okay?"

"Yeah, it was scary, but I came through it," she said.

"Detective, you see a connection between everything that's happened?" Rod asked.

Preston nodded. "The one thing you and Abby have in common is Carl. There's a link somewhere, and I'm going to find it."

"Carl and I liked playing one-on-one on the basketball slab here on the estate. Afterward, we'd down a few cold ones. That's the extent of our friendship," he said. "As for this shooter today, I'm thinking that maybe he followed *you* here."

"Me? What makes you think that? He was moving right for you," Preston said.

"This kind of thing doesn't happen to me, dude. People in this community like me," he said. "I keep thinking of a TV show I saw last night, a suicide-by-cop thing. The guy's life was going down the toilet, but he didn't have the guts to kill himself. He set it up by taking a hostage and waving around a gun so the cops would have to shoot him."

"That's what you think happened here?"

"Yeah, he pulled his gun and aimed at me, but then you screwed up his plan by not taking him out. Are you sure his gun was even loaded?"

"It was," Preston said. He started to point out that no one had followed him to the estate either when Abby rose to her feet, her eyes sparking with anger.

"I know you don't like cops, and you're having a tough time saying thank you," she said, resting her arms on the edge of

Rod's desk, leaning forward and looking directly at the big man. "But the detective saved your life and you're sounding like an ungrateful horse's butt. You owe him. Now get over it, and say thank you."

Rod cracked a slow smile. "A horse's butt?"

"You heard me," she said, not backing down.

Rod shrugged and extended his hand. "Sorry, dude. You came through for me so thanks. I get anxious around cops. Knee-jerk reaction from my days back in Jersey. I think it's an allergy," he said with the wide smile that was as much a part of his trademark as his outrageous personality.

"I'm glad I was in a position to help." Preston shook his hand.

"We're going to have to work together so things can get back to normal at the ranch," Abby said. "I need to open our doors again as soon as possible."

"How can I help?" Rod asked.

"You can cooperate with the detective…and if it's not too much to ask for right now, we could sure use a donation to our barn roof fund. With the economy still so weak—"

He held up a hand, interrupting her. "Ilse!" he bellowed.

The woman came back in instantly.

"Cut a check for a barn roof."

"Amount?" she asked, looking at Abby.

Abby gave her the estimate, then quickly added, "I know that's high, so whatever amount Rod can afford will help."

"Give her the entire amount," Rod said.

"Thank you so much!"

"Abby, when Stretch Jackson's kid was diagnosed with cancer, you and the ranch helped give that little girl something to smile about. You let her ride the camels and that was all she talked about till she passed away. I told you back then that I wouldn't forget. So whatever you need, come to me. If I can't get it, I'll help you raise the cash."

"Your support means the world to us, Rod. Thanks again."

"Now tell me how I can help your investigation," Rod said.

"I need to fill in some of the blanks in Carl's life," Preston said. "You knew him, so maybe you could tell me about Carl's gambling habits and who he met when he went to the casino."

"Dawg, you're way off the mark. Carl was no gambler. He'd only go to the casino when the ranch was working a promo there or when he was promised a free meal. After playing one-to-one here, we'd clean up, cool down, then head over there for dinner."

"How often did you two get together?" Preston asked.

"Two, sometimes three times a week. I'm six foot eight so it was nearly impossible for me to find anyone willing to play pick-up ball. Then I met Carl. Nothing intimidated the guy. He was only six foot two, but he was fast and lean. He'd played basketball in high school and loved the game."

"So how long have you two been friends?" Preston asked.

"About two years. I'd seen him trying to rig up a goal on a light pole over by the bunkhouse, so I told him to forget it and come over here. I've got goals indoors and out. He and I hit it off from the start. We'd play hard outdoors, like back in the 'hood, then when the weather was bad, in my gym."

"What else can you tell me about Carl? Did he worry about anything in particular? Did he tend to look over his shoulder a lot, like someone who knew he was a target? Anything that comes to mind might help."

"Dude, we didn't get into that touchy-feely stuff. We played basketball. The guy had good moves on the court—I can tell you that—plus an old-school hook shot that was accurate and hard to block."

"When you went to the casino, was he more comfortable playing the slots than the game tables?" It was an old interrogation technique. You stated something as a fact, then waited for the response.

"B-man, aren't you listening?" he said, coming up with a nickname for Preston. "Carl didn't gamble. He watched me play a few hands of poker one time, but he wasn't interested, even when I offered to cover him. As for the slots, he told me that it was a game for suckers."

"So besides basketball, what else did Carl like to do?"

"Sketching and painting. He told me he'd lived hard and fast all his life, and it was time for him to slow down. He also loved working with animals."

"Rod, here's the thing. I found some slot machine tickets at the bunkhouse. If Carl didn't put them there, they might have been left by his killer," Preston said. "The quickest way for me to rule out Carl and maybe identify a possible suspect is to check surveillance tapes at the casino. Problem is, I don't have a court order, and there's no way I can get one based on what I have. Can you help me cut a few corners by speaking to their head of security? It'll speed up the investigation."

Rod shook his head slowly. "I can't help you there, B-man. Had you asked me a few weeks ago, maybe. I owned quite a few shares in the casino, but I had to sell them to cover some bad investments. I can talk to some of their people, but my word doesn't carry any weight there now."

Though she'd been pretty quiet till now, Abby spoke. "Until this case is closed, I can't reopen the ranch, and our reputation will continue to take a hit. By helping Detective Bowman, you'd be helping us, too."

Rod expelled his breath in a hiss. "Okay, I'll see what I can do, but I ain't promising anything. You hear?"

"Loud and clear." Preston stood and Rod shook his hand. "One more thing. Gorman is being booked right now, but I'd like both of you to go to the station with me and make an official statement."

"I'll follow you there," Abby said.

"I'll get my attorney first, then meet you there," Rod said. "Me and the police…not a good combination."

Preston bit back a smile.

Abby followed Preston outside. "Carl really cared about the ranch and he worked hard. Whenever I needed something done, he took care of it without a question. You're investigating the murder as if it's Carl's fault somehow, but he was one of the good guys."

"Even a good person can have secrets." He said it mostly to see what her reaction would be.

Abby averted her gaze and, promising to meet him at the station, walked away quickly.

"You're hiding something, pretty lady, and that's a bad idea," he murmured, his words nothing more than a whisper in the wind.

Chapter Eight

After giving her statement, Abby waited alone in Preston's office. Restless, she paced the small, windowless room, trying to learn more about him. There were no personal photos on his desk and the only thing on the wall was a commendation for bravery. It was framed but hung in a section of the wall that was partially hidden each time the door was open, as it was now.

All she really knew about Preston was what she'd learned from doing an online search using her cell phone. Last year, he'd stopped a robbery in progress. He'd been at the bank on personal business at the time and had subdued and handcuffed the armed suspect before anyone was hurt.

Preston appeared to be as dedicated to his job as she was to her ranch. He was cool under pressure and accomplished whatever he set out to do, but there was another side to him, too. She'd seen glimpses of it in the way he'd treated Bobby and the gentle strength he'd shown her when he'd held her after that man had tried to run her down. Intuition told her that beyond the badge lay a man of passion whose feelings ran deep and strong.

She shook her head, exasperated with herself, and tried to think clearly. She'd been nearly hysterical, about to be run over, and under the circumstances any overreaction to a place of safety was understandable.

Preston came in just then, and the total absence of emotion on his face warned her that something bad was coming.

"Please sit down," he said coldly. "The clerk will bring in your statement shortly. You can read it over, make any corrections, then sign it."

"Then I can leave?" She wasn't sure why she'd asked that, except maybe to make sure she would be free to go.

"We need to discuss something first."

Here it was. Somehow, even before he spoke, she knew he'd found out.

"The crime scene investigators have processed the evidence, and a few important facts about Carl have come up."

Abby said nothing. She wasn't sure how much he knew, and she figured she'd be better off not speaking at all.

Preston remained quiet, allowing the seconds to stretch out.

Abby squirmed. The total silence between them was completely disconcerting. She stared at her lap, then with effort made herself look directly at him. "Some secrets are meant to be shared, but others deserve respect."

"Your logic doesn't apply to a murder investigation."

"This is the first time I've ever dealt with a murder, so you'll have to forgive me if I don't know the rules," she shot back, then cringed when he didn't react at all.

"You knew Carl had a criminal record."

It wasn't a question. She exhaled loudly. "Yes. His real name is...was...Carl Sinclair, not Woods."

"Did you think we wouldn't find out?"

"No, quite the opposite. I knew you would, and that's why I waited," she said. "When Carl came to me asking for a job, he told me the truth about himself. He'd grown up in Hartley, then moved to Denver, San Francisco and other cities, where he made a living as an art thief. Eventually he got caught and served his time. He swore he was clean now and asked that

I let him prove himself. I ran a background check, like I do with everyone who works at the ranch, and the investigator verified Carl's story. After that, I knew I could trust Carl. As badly as he'd wanted a second chance, he didn't come to me under false pretenses."

"He served time for burglary—four years to be exact."

"I know. He learned to work with horses while in prison, but then you know all that already. What you probably don't know is how good he was with animals. They responded to him in a way that was nothing short of amazing. You may have found out about Carl's past, but you know very little about the man he became. Carl worked hard to make the most out of the chance I gave him. That's why I'd like people to remember Carl Woods, the man he was at the time of his death, not Carl Sinclair, the man he'd been a long time ago. Can you keep all this private?"

"I'll try, but information like this has a way of getting out."

"People won't understand," she said with a tired sigh. "I don't care what they think about me. I know I did the right thing hiring him. I'm just afraid that it'll hurt the ranch."

"Some will use Carl's past against you, but don't underestimate the public. Many will side with your decision to give Carl a chance," he said. "Giving folks a hand up is what you do every day at the ranch, Abby. Look at Bobby. The world sees a handicapped Navajo kid, but you don't accept that definition, so Bobby doesn't either. What you did for him was force him to redefine normal."

"He did that on his own. Bobby's super smart."

The clerk came into the room with Abby's statement and placed it on Preston's desk.

He was quiet until the woman left, then met Abby's gaze and held it. "Remember one thing, Abby. You want answers and so do I. No more secrets. Don't make my job harder than it already is."

Abby read her statement and then signed it. "If you don't need me anymore I should get back to the ranch. I have to take care of the animals, then hit the sack. I'll have to be up early for a staff meeting. I want them to hear about Carl from me first, not pick up some distorted gossip around town."

Preston stood when Abby did, ready to walk her to the door, when he saw Rod Garner striding down the hall toward his office.

"Did you find out anything new about the guy who came after me?" Rod asked, stepping into the room.

Preston nodded. "It turns out the casino hired away the cook at his restaurant, the Night Owl Café. Business started to suffer and Gorman couldn't find another chef good enough to keep his regular customers. He went out of business and blames you because he found out that you recommended his former cook to the casino."

"I remember the café," Rod said, nodding slowly. "The chef there was very good. Since the meals at the casino were just average, I told the restaurant manager about the guy. I had no idea what happened after that."

"Gorman has other problems, too, including substance abuse, so it was just a matter of time. One of the reasons his chef quit was because he wasn't getting a regular paycheck. Gorman was on a downward spiral. He'll at least have a chance to get clean in jail. They have a rehab program now," Preston added. "On the surface it doesn't look like there's a connection to Carl."

"But you're still not convinced?" Rod asked.

"Let's just say I'm keeping an open mind," Preston said.

As Abby walked away down the hall, she received a call from Michelle, who was at the ranch.

"I thought you'd want to know that we've received the horse Gene Redhouse donated. Kyle Goodluck, Detective Bowman's brother, just dropped him off."

"We have a stall in the barn prepared for Red, so put him in there and let him get settled. Could you come in early tomorrow? We need to hold a meeting. Tell the volunteers who are there tonight to come, too, if they can. I'll call the rest of our regulars once I get back."

As Abby headed to her truck, she thought about tomorrow's meeting. Would they continue to respect her judgment or lose faith in her, thinking she was unrealistic and a hopeless optimist? Yet, it was precisely her ability to believe in people and herself that had helped make the ranch a reality.

As she thought of her staff, Abby turned and walked back to the station. She could use some support. Moments later, she found Preston still in his office at his computer.

"I'd like to ask you a favor," she said as she knocked on the open door.

He waved at her to have a seat. "Sure. What's on your mind?"

"Would you come to the ranch tomorrow morning, say, seven? I'd like you to tell the staff about Carl—that he'd paid his dues and hadn't been in trouble since. As a cop, that'll carry more weight coming from you," she said and explained why she was concerned. "To believe in the ranch, they need to trust me."

He met her gaze and held it. For a moment it felt as if he were looking straight into her soul. Did he feel the magic building between them? Did he know the way he affected her?

After what seemed like an eternity, he nodded. "All right."

Hearing a commotion outside, he stood. "Come on, I'll walk you out. It sounds like one of our uniforms is bringing in someone who has had too much to drink."

She fell into step beside him as they crossed the parking lot. "My work has some very sad moments but, by and large, it's about making things better. Things stay upbeat most of the time," she said. "Your work has got to be so much harder than mine. How do you deal with the pressure that comes with being a homicide cop?"

"To me, it's all about preserving the balance between good and evil. As a Navajo, I believe that everything has two sides. Evil needs good to define it, and good is needed to keep evil in check. I'm here to make sure harmony is restored."

As they reached her truck, she glanced over at him. Preston stood tall, his wide shoulders thrown back. Everything about him was solid and unwavering. No matter how tough the circumstances, he was the kind of man who could be relied on.

There was just something about him that inspired confidence and as she looked at him, she knew the future of her ranch was in good hands.

PRESTON SET OUT to Abby's first thing the following morning. He was nearly there when Gabe Sanchez from the crime scene unit called.

"You're at it early," Preston said.

"Figured you'd want answers as soon as possible."

"You got that right."

"I've got preliminaries for you," Gabe said. "There were traces of the vic's blood and hair on the blade of a shovel we found near the barn, but the absence of blood in the horse pen tends to indicate that he wasn't killed there. He was struck somewhere else, then moved to that corral afterward."

"Yeah, that matches up with the fact that someone went to a lot of trouble to hide his or her footprints."

"We also checked the gambling tokens and tickets you found. The prints were smudged, but the few identifying characteristics we found didn't match the vic's."

"Interesting. Looks like the killer may have planted those. It's possible Carl may have been killed around the bunkhouse, judging from the time of death, then moved to the pen to mislead the investigation. The extra blood could have been scooped up and buried somewhere else," Preston said. "It's time for me to take a closer look at the staff. This may have been an inside job."

As Preston hung up, he considered the possibility that Abby had an enemy in her ranks. The killer could be someone she trusted, and that was bound to make things tougher. Her fierce loyalty to her staff, judging by the way she'd kept Carl's secret, might blind her to danger.

Abby was more vulnerable than she realized. As a homicide cop, he worked long hours and spent a lot of time alone, but his brothers were there for him, day or night, and just a phone call away. From what he'd seen, Abby had no close friends or family.

Preston prided himself on being a tough cop, as hard as any on the force, and that was because he never brought emotions into the picture. As he pulled into Sitting Tall Ranch and saw Abby stop to pet a horse, something told him that was all about to change.

WHILE THE STAFF gathered for the meeting, which had been delayed ten minutes, Preston saw his brother Kyle standing just inside the office door.

Preston took him aside. "Did you decide to volunteer here?"

"Yeah. I came by this morning to check on Red and offer my services. I figured you could use an additional pair of eyes and ears here. I've already introduced myself to some of the volunteers and met an accountant named Stan Cooper. Turns out Stan didn't care for Carl at all. He said the man worked hard, but there was something about him he never trusted."

"Interesting," Preston said.

Just then Abby stepped to the front of the room. Preston and Kyle stayed back, keeping an eye on the others gathered there.

"We all have private lives," Abby said, telling them about Carl's past. "Carl told me who he really was and asked for a chance to prove himself. I gave him one and he never let me down."

As Preston stepped forward all eyes turned to him. "Ms. Langdon is right about Carl. From everything I've been able to find out, the man had cleaned up his act. It's important to remember, too, that he was the victim of a crime, not the perpetrator."

After Preston finished speaking, a photo of Carl appeared on the small TV screen in the corner of the room. The sound had been muted, but Michelle, who'd obviously glanced over, pointed. "Hey, look! What's that all about?"

Abby turned up the volume, stepped back and listened to Marsha Robertson's news segment.

"Though well liked and respected at Sitting Tall Ranch, where he took care of the animals, it appears that Carl Woods, aka Carl Sinclair, had a hidden past. Our source has verified that he was a convicted art thief who served a four-year prison sentence. There's speculation that Sinclair may have been keeping other secrets which might have led to his murder."

"How did they find out so soon?" Abby asked, looking back at Preston.

"I was afraid this would happen," he said. "I saw Marsha Robertson at the station earlier. She has sources everywhere."

Abby sat down on the corner of her desk and faced the gathering. "Although this is bound to make things worse, you should all know that the backlash against the ranch started even before that news segment. I checked my email first thing this morning and found out that the 4-H kids who volunteer here won't be returning for a while. Their parents and the 4-H sponsors are insisting they stay away until this matter is resolved. That means we'll have to set up new feeding schedules and split up the work among the rest of us."

Preston nodded, pleased with her reaction. Though kicked while down, she'd gotten right back up. She was a fighter. All she needed was a hand, and he intended to do all he could to help her.

Chapter Nine

After the staff meeting was over, Michelle came up to Abby. "Can I talk to you privately for a moment?"

Somehow this sounded like more bad news. Ignoring the knot in her stomach, Abby smiled. "Sure. What's up?"

"I've had some cash flow problems lately and I'm behind on some of my bills. Miller's Horse Farm won't let me use their facilities until I get caught up, so I'd like to make you a trade. I'll add fifteen volunteer hours to my regular work schedule here if you'll let me use one of the arenas for my weekly riding classes. I'll work around the ranch's schedule, of course."

"I could use the help, so it sounds doable," she said, "but there's something I need to know. How come you're in trouble financially? What happened?"

"It's nothing bad, Abby, so don't worry. I just got in over my head when I bought a new horse trailer. Now the payments are eating me alive."

Abby smiled. "Okay. I was that way, too, when I started buying tack for the animals."

As they walked outside, Abby heard the sound of a big engine in the parking lot. A tow truck was backing up to the ranch's pickup, and two men were standing by the driver's-side door, which was open.

"Hey! Get away from my truck!" Abby yelled, then broke into a run.

Abby heard footsteps behind her. Turning her head for a second she saw Preston almost catching up to her. Michelle was right behind him.

"What's going on?" Preston asked, matching her speed.

"Those men are trying to steal my truck!"

He slowed to a walk as they approached the tow truck. "These guys are from a repo company, Abby. You behind on your payments?"

"No chance," Abby said. "Stan handles all those details for me and he would have told me if there was a problem."

"Hang back and let me check things out for you. These guys are trouble. I've been called to deal with them before," Preston said.

Kyle came up beside him. "Got your back, bro."

Preston went to the men by the tow truck. "Before you hook anything up, let me see your paperwork."

"Butt out, Indian. The lady's a freeloader. She's missed three loan payments in a row, and we're duly authorized to take the truck." He waved a manila folder full of papers.

"That's just not true," Abby said, her hands on her hips. "If there had been a problem, the bank would have notified the ranch. You've got the wrong address and the wrong truck."

"Save the story, lady. We've heard it all," the big guy said. The other two men came around to stand beside him. One was holding a length of tow chain.

"I'm telling you the truth—and you're not taking my truck," Abby said, stepping up to the man. "There's been some kind of mistake. Let me talk to the bank. I'm sure I can clear this up in five minutes." She reached out for the folder, but he pulled it away.

"Too late. We're taking the pickup. Next time make your

payments," he said, then laughed and threw the folder full of papers at her.

"I'm a police officer," Preston said, instantly getting into the man's face.

The two other men stepped forward. One tried to grab Preston by the arm, but Kyle hurled himself at the guy, tackling him to the ground.

As they fought, the other guy took a swing at Preston. Blocking the punch, Preston grabbed the man's extended arm and bent it inward at the elbow until the guy fell to his knees in agony.

The big guy took advantage of the situation and grabbed Abby, holding her arms by the wrists far enough away so she couldn't kick him. Abby tried to twist free, but he tightened his hold.

"Back off, you two," he snapped. "Let go of my crew."

Preston held his hands up and stepped back, then suddenly shoved the guy he'd been fighting in the chest with the palm of his hand, knocking him straight into the leader. As the two collided, Abby twisted free and the big man fell to the ground.

Kyle still had the third guy pinned, but the one Preston had shoved whirled around, throwing a roundhouse punch. Preston ducked, kneed the man in the groin and drew his weapon before the leader could react.

"You're all under arrest," Preston snapped. "Down on your knees."

"We are within our rights taking this truck," the leader said, putting his hands in the air.

"We'll have to verify that. But whatever the case, you've assaulted a police officer and a civilian, a woman half your size. You're facing charges, so don't push your luck."

"There are two patrol officers on the way," Abby said, holding up her cell phone, signaling she'd dialed 911.

Preston and Kyle, intending to turn the trio over to the uniformed cops when they arrived, escorted the men to the front gate. The suspect in handcuffs led the way while the other two, hands locked behind their heads, followed.

"Consider carrying extra sets of cuffs while you're working this case, bro," Kyle said.

"I'll keep that in mind."

After the men were taken to the station, Preston went to Abby's office. She was just hanging up the phone. "I spoke to Stan. He said it was a glitch in the software. He's got an automatic payment set up, but he thinks it may have gone into someone else's account. He'll get things straightened out in the next hour or so."

"Abby, what were you thinking?" Preston demanded. "You shouldn't have argued with that guy. He outweighed you by at least one hundred pounds."

"I knew you'd be there to back me up. You asked me to trust you, remember?" she asked. "So I did."

"She's got your number," Kyle said, chuckling.

PRESTON stood alone with Kyle in the nearly empty bull pen at the station. It was close to noon now and Abby was still giving her statement to the clerk.

"So what's the deal with you and Abby Langdon? Are you seriously interested in her?" Kyle asked.

"No interest other than professional. She needs a hand and I'm in a position to help. Nothing more."

"Why don't I believe you?"

Preston started to answer when Abby came up to him. "May I speak to you for a moment?"

"Sure," he said, then glanced back at Kyle. "Thanks for the help, bro."

"No problem," Kyle said and strode off.

"All the paperwork is done and I've signed my statement,"

Abby said as they walked down the hall toward Preston's office.

"Good. You won't be seeing those guys again anytime soon. They'll be spending the night in jail, then they'll be facing a judge tomorrow."

"That's one less worry for me tonight," she said.

"What's bothering you?"

"I've been wondering if it's really safe for me to stay at the ranch alone at night. If I'm sound asleep, I may not hear a problem until it's too late. The killer is still out there."

The worried smile she gave him tore at his guts.

"I'm not a coward," she added quickly.

"I know you're not. You're just dealing with something that's part of my world, not yours."

"I've faced tough situations before but never anything like this." She shook her head. "How do I handle it?"

"Step back and don't let things overwhelm you. I'll find the killer. That's what I do best."

Seeing her shudder, he had to fight the urge to pull her into his arms. They were at the station and acting on that urge was a bad idea. What he could do was keep her company for a little longer.

"I'm going to grab a hamburger across the street," he said. "Join me?"

She glanced at her watch and shook her head. "I'd like to, but I've got to go back. I have to meet with Stan and go over the quarterly reports." She paused, then smiled. "But here's what I can do. Why don't you meet me this evening for dinner? I make one mean green chile cheeseburger and it'll be my way of saying thanks for being there for me today."

"Just doing my job," he said.

"No, you've gone above and beyond."

As she looked up and he saw himself reflected in the softness of her eyes, heat flashed through him, hot and strong.

"Okay, I'll tell you what. I'll come early, help you with the livestock, then we'll eat," he said, trying to get his mind back on the right track. He didn't need physical distractions like this. Entanglements had never turned out well for him, probably because he didn't trust the emotions that went along with them.

"Can I recruit your help fixing dinner, too?"

He laughed. "Hey, I think I'm getting a raw deal there."

"Nah, I just want you to help me make sure there are no leftovers," she said with a smile.

"Then I'm your man." As he spoke, he knew instantly that it had been a poor choice of words. Something flashed in her eyes and the attraction between them surged to a new level. What the hell was he getting into?

Chapter Ten

The rest of the day had gone by quickly. Stan had straightened things with the bank and had made out their proposed quarterly budget. If donations didn't hold steady, things promised to get tough.

Now, working side by side with Preston, Abby was in a far better mood. They'd finished refilling the horses' water troughs and were walking back to the main house, her home, as darkness finally descended over the ranch.

"You look tired," he said.

"I am, but physical work helps me unwind. When I'm tired I also tend not to worry so much. I'm a great one for waking up at three in the morning and stewing over a million what-ifs."

"Trying to head off problems is a good strategy, but endless worrying is not."

"I know, but sometimes I just can't help it."

It was honest and to the point, like she was. "Do you ever regret dedicating so much of your life to this place?"

She took a deep breath. "Sometimes I wonder what my life would have been like if I'd made more traditional choices. As it is, I rarely date, and my private life is practically nonexistent, but the ranch does give me something in return. I have a very special family here. The children's faces change often, but what we share at the ranch connects us forever."

"Dedication—to anything—always carries a price," he

said. "A lot of women have come and gone in my life, but the truth is, I'm married to police work."

She smiled. The similarities between them only heightened her attraction to him. It was all very unsettling—but undeniably exciting. "Doing what we're meant to do is satisfying, but it can also be lonely at times."

"Maybe so, but I've got family nearby. Most of my brothers live in this area. What about your family?"

"After my sister passed away, Mom and Dad were heartbroken. They both died within a year, one right after the other," she said. After a long pause, she continued. "Watching someone you love die a little each day breaks your heart in a way that never quite heals. Sandy was my fraternal twin and a part of us was connected. For a long time after her death, I was lost. Nothing made sense to me. If everything could be taken from you at any given moment, why bother doing anything at all? I'm not sure if there is a hell, but that's as close to it as I've ever found."

"So how did this ranch come about?"

"When Sandy started going downhill, the thing she wanted to do most of all was go horseback riding. She loved horses, but we didn't own any. I tried finding someone who'd let her ride, but people were worried about liability if something went wrong. I finally got a local rancher to agree and the difference that outing made in Sandy was amazing. For a few hours she got to do something *she* wanted. She died in peace a few weeks after that." She swallowed hard. "Wherever she is, I'm sure she's on a horse," she added with a sad smile.

Her sorrow stabbed through him. He remembered what it was like when he'd found himself alone so many years back. Goodbye could be the cruelest words of all time, especially coming from the most important person in your life.

Although he wanted to pull her into his arms and comfort her, she moved back and shook her head.

"I'm fine. Memories can hurt, but we go on," she said in a slightly steadier tone. "I'll always miss her, but it's thanks to her that this ranch was founded. Her spirit lives on here."

He reached for her hand and gave it a gentle squeeze. "Did the idea for the ranch come to you right away?"

"Not immediately, no, but as time wore on, I saw that a ranch like this one would be the perfect way to honor her life. We may not be able to change our final destination, but we can make the most out of the time we've got," she said, stopping to give the horses a few carrots. "My dream was to create an extraordinary ranch for kids facing major challenges." She looked at him and smiled sheepishly. "The problem was that I was nineteen at the time and had no money."

"So you got donations and sold your idea to a bank?"

"Eventually, yes, but first I needed capital of my own," she said. "I opened up an employment agency that provided skilled workers for small or large construction projects anywhere in the state. My business grew quickly, and three years later I sold it. I made enough of a profit to buy this ranch, but I still needed investors who could share my vision. Helping Sitting Tall Ranch become what it is today took time and a lot of effort." She looked around her and smiled. "Mostly, it was about never taking no for an answer."

As she moved away from the horse pen, a camel roared, spooking the horses.

"That's Hank. Something or someone he doesn't know or like is moving around over by his enclosure."

He started to reach for his gun, but she shook her head. "It might just be a stray dog. Hank's more vocal and territorial than your typical camel. He lets everyone know if he sees something that's out of place or different somehow."

"That's a really loud call. Did he do that the night Carl died?" Preston asked.

She blinked. "He might have, but although we didn't get any rain, we had some pretty loud thunder that night."

"I'm going to check it out."

"I'm going with you," she said.

"Stay behind me then," he said, heading back to the camel pen.

Both camels were at the far end of their welded pipe enclosure, less than fifty feet from the bunkhouse.

Abby nudged Preston and gestured to a small beam of light just outside the rear of the bunkhouse.

"I'll handle it," he whispered, reaching for his gun. "Stay back."

As he crept forward, Abby caught a glimpse of the intruder's face. "Wait, Preston. That's one of the high school kids who volunteers here."

Abby immediately strode toward the teen, who was standing in the open and illuminated by the full moon overhead. "Norman, what on earth are you doing here skulking around like this? And who's that with you?" she added, seeing a shadow a few feet away.

"It's me, Abby. Don't be angry," another familiar voice said.

"Meet Norman and Jenny Rager," she told Preston, then focused back on the pair. "Tell me what you're doing here?"

"It was so much money! And we would have split it with you," Norman said. "Honest!"

"You've lost me," Abby said.

"*The Inquisitor,* the statewide tabloid, is offering two hundred bucks for a photo of the bunkhouse and the stall where the body was found."

"It wasn't just for the money, Abby," Jenny said. "People are saying that Carl was just another crook with a good line and you fell for his story. We figured that if everyone could see where he lived, how simple his life was, they'd realize Carl was just a regular hardworking guy."

"And we didn't break in," Norman added quickly. "The gate was open and we parked in the parking area. You weren't around, so we came back here."

"You're still trespassing," Preston said sharply.

"I'm going to let this go," Abby said with a sigh. "But if either of you pull something like this again, I'll press charges. Clear?"

"Clear!" Norman said, then hurried back with his sister Jenny toward the parking lot.

"If that 'bloid is offering money for photos, this could get ugly," Preston said.

"I'll make some calls tomorrow morning and see if I can get them to stop. I know some people."

By the time the kids had left and they were back at the ranch house, Abby was exhausted. "Come in. I promised you dinner, and by now you're probably starving."

"Yeah, but you're beat. I can see it on your face. Let me take a rain check."

"Are you sure?"

"Yeah. I can head back to the station and check out a few things."

"Like the tabloid photo offer?"

He nodded. "But I think that's just routine for the tabloid. Anytime there's a local story like this they like to sensationalize it. That's how they sell papers," he said. "One more thing before I leave, Abby. Consider installing security cameras."

"I don't know about that," she said slowly. "If I do, it might worry people even more. I'd be publicly acknowledging that I believe the ranch is no longer safe. Keep in mind that my battle will be fought—and won or lost—in the court of public opinion. A move like that could work against me."

He nodded slowly. "There's one thing you need to consider—the fact that you never heard Hank roar the night Carl was killed could mean it was an inside job."

"No. I know my people. No one who works for me could have done something like that. It's more likely that the killer came in from a different direction and avoided Hank's enclosure altogether."

Preston held her gaze. "I know you want to believe that, but you have to stay open to the possibility. Until we know for sure, stay alert and don't lower your guard," he said. "Will you be hiring someone to take Carl's place?"

"Not right away," she said. "It takes forever to find someone who's willing to work very long hours for a flat rate in exchange for living quarters."

"I'll help you spread the word. Maybe someone at the station will have a retired relative or know of someone who's good with animals, like an old cowboy."

"Thanks. I appreciate that." Before she could say anything more, they heard Hank's ponderous groan. "Again?"

"Maybe someone besides Norman and Jenny got the same idea. Wait here," Preston said, holding up his hand.

As he ran off, she remained behind for a moment, then changed her mind. Though Preston was a well-trained police officer, everyone could use a hand now and then. Years of moving eighty-pound hay bales had given her incredible strength to put into a right hook. Or she could give an attacker a boot kick in the shins, if it came to that.

Chapter Eleven

Preston saw a shadowy figure creeping around the barn. All the animals seemed agitated. Judging from the shape and the way the suspect moved, the person was male and was wearing a dark-colored hoodie. In the bright moonlight he could see that the tall, broad-shouldered man was spray painting graffiti on the side of the barn.

"Police! Don't move!" Preston called out.

The man took off instantly, running at full speed. Preston was fast, but by the time he reached the road, the man was racing away on a motorcycle. He was too far away for Preston to get a plate ID or even the make of the machine.

Preston called it in. "I won't catch him now," he said as Abby caught up to him. "I should have waited until I got closer before I said anything. He's heading back to the highway, so tracking him now is not a possibility."

She shone her flashlight on the side of the barn. "What's that supposed to mean?" The drawing depicted a stick figure inside a circle with a diagonal line across it. "I don't understand. What's he saying? No stick figures? No art? Wait—no people, no kids?"

"Probably," Preston said and took photos of it with his cell phone. "Unless you have some paint solvent, you should cover this over before anyone arrives tomorrow morning. Don't give the tagger the satisfaction of having others see his work."

"I have a gallon of barn-red paint left over for touch-ups. It'll cover in one coat and won't take long."

By the time she came back out with paint, tools and a battery-powered lantern, Preston had taken off his jacket and bolo tie and placed them over the top rail of the fence.

She smiled, set down the paint can and a cardboard box, then turned on the lantern. "You're not dressed for this. I'll take care of it. Once I get the paint all stirred and in the tray, I'll just need a few minutes. I've got a big roller and years of experience painting exterior walls."

"So do I, so count me in. You get the paint mixed while I take off my shirt." He saw her stealing quick glances as he hung his shirt next to his jacket. The first time it was curiosity. After that, it was because she liked what she saw. Biting back a smile, he got to work.

THOUGH SHE TRIED not to get caught looking at him, she couldn't help sneaking a few glances at Preston. His strong shoulders and bronzed arms rippled with muscles as he moved the roller in diagonal and vertical strokes, applying the paint.

As he bent down to replenish the roller, she checked out his lower half and had to bite back a sigh. He was a living, breathing temptation.

"Like what you see?" he asked without even looking back.

"How did you know—" She pressed her lips together and glanced away. "Wow. Walked right into that, didn't I?"

He laughed, then turned around to face her. "No harm in looking," he said, then allowed his gaze to take her in from top to bottom slowly.

Heat, the kind that teased and tantalized, spread all through her, but she managed to hold back a shiver of pleasure. He'd seen way too much already in her expression.

They finished painting quickly, then washed the tray and roller in a big utility sink inside the barn.

"Okay, we're done here. Let's head back to the house. The least I can do to say thank-you is microwave us a frozen pizza."

He removed the latex gloves she'd provided, then before reaching for his shirt, noticed a paint smudge on his chest and tried to rub it off with his hand.

"Let me get that," Abby said, moistening a hand towel with water.

She came up to him. "Hold still for a sec. The paint's water-based, but now's the time to wipe it off."

As she stood close, she became aware of everything about him. The heat from his body enveloped her, sparking her senses. Her hand began to tremble as she wiped the paint away.

"No need to be nervous," he said, wrapping his arms around her waist and pulling her against him.

As she looked up into his eyes, she saw the fire there and her breath caught in her throat. She should have stepped away, but everything feminine in her demanded she stay. Abby wrapped her arms around him and shivered as he nuzzled her neck, leaving a trail of moist kisses there.

She pressed herself against him, wanting more, and as she drew in a breath, his mouth closed over hers. The kiss was slow and deep, then grew more demanding with each passing second.

He drew back, taking a breath, but she brought his lips back to hers, unwilling to have it end so soon.

He lowered his hand to her bottom and pressed her against him, letting her feel his hardness.

Knowing she was desired heightened her pleasure but soon it became too hot. Fighting herself, she took an unsteady step back.

He released his hold on her but stood his ground, his chest heaving, his eyes still gleaming with a dark fire. "Sorry."

"No, don't be. It was…wonderful. But we had to stop."

One-night stands, however tempting, weren't for her. After the passion cooled, they only made her feel emotionally drained and more alone than ever.

"Come on," she said, picking up her flashlight, which had been resting on the fence post. "With everything's that happened, we're too wired to rest. Let's have dinner."

"I was hoping for dessert first," he said with a crooked grin.

She laughed. "Will you settle for three-cheese pizza and some beer?"

He raised his eyebrows in surprise. "You didn't strike me as the kind who'd have beer in the fridge."

"Busted," she said, chuckling. "I've had the same six-pack in there since our staff's last monthly get-together. It's one Saturday a month and very informal. Basically, we grill hamburgers and everyone brings something—potluck style."

Once they'd reached the main house she led him into the living room. The old ranch house was decorated southwestern style with a leather couch, two chairs and a wool area rug over brick flooring. The walls held various "before and after" shots of the ranch.

He accepted the cold beer she handed him—a local brew.

Abby took a box of pizza out of the freezer and placed the contents onto the bottom of the box atop the silver heating surface. "I can add some green chile to it so it's a New Mexican pizza. You game?"

"Always," he said.

As their eyes met, she felt a prickle of excitement. Preston was all about self-control and restraint, a police officer through and through, but when he'd held her, she'd caught a glimpse of the rough, powerful man he kept tightly leashed.

She bit back a sigh and looked away. She had to get her thoughts back onto safer channels. Why was she making such a fuss over a kiss or two? This just wasn't like her.

"The living room's nice, but it doesn't say much about you or your style. Is that intentional?"

She started the microwave, then glanced back at him. "You're right and, yes, it's intentional."

He waited and didn't interrupt the silence.

"To build a dream, you have to be able to weather a lot of disappointments. That requires some separation between the dream and the dreamer." The microwave dinged and she pulled out the pizza. "I sometimes bring donors into my living room and entertain there. The rest of the house is just for me—a place where I can retreat from the worries of every day. My favorite room is one I converted into a small library. It's filled with romance and fantasy novels."

"I would have said those two are the same," he answered with a grin as they ate. "Isn't fantasizing part of romance?"

She laughed. "You tell me," she said, meeting his gaze and holding it.

She'd only meant it as a playful, subtle challenge, but when he didn't look away, she felt a stirring inside her, a yearning for what simply wasn't meant to be.

"Another beer?" she asked, going to the fridge just to put some distance between them.

"No, I'm good."

By the time she joined him at the table, she felt more in control. "You clearly know your way around women, Preston, and when you want company it's a safe bet that there's no shortage of volunteers. But I think you should know that I can't handle casual flings. I'm just not built that way," she said as they finished eating.

He leaned forward and tucked a loose strand of hair behind her ear.

He never said a word, yet that one fleeting touch sent shock waves all through her. She stood and took their plates to the sink. More than anything, she wished she could jump back into his arms and kiss him again. She'd almost forgotten what it was like to feel desired and so deliciously and powerfully feminine.

As she gazed out her kitchen window at the barn, she took a deep breath, composing herself. She had to stay focused on the ranch and keep the terrible thing that had happened from harming it.

"Carl's death was a devastating blow, but now the ranch is becoming a target, too. I realize that tagging and those dumb emails are just minor annoyances in comparison to what's already happened, but when is this going to stop?"

"Wait—what emails?"

"It's nothing, just nuisance letters."

"Show me what you're talking about."

"They started showing up in my inbox a few hours after we found Carl's body. I've deleted most of them, but by now there's bound to be some more there."

"Let me take a look."

She walked to the hallway, then stopped and glanced back at him. "I don't have a laptop, so we'll have to go into my home office. That's where I keep my personal PC."

"The part of your house you don't like people to see," he said with a nod. "Don't worry. I'll keep your secrets." His slow smile was full of mischief. "Let's see…you're a hoarder? You have a collection of overdue library books stacked ceiling high. They're in rows, with just a narrow aisle in the middle."

She laughed. "You're a bonehead."

"A what?"

"Forget it. Follow me," she said. Although she knew Preston was just trying to set her at ease, she wished she hadn't had to bring him back here. He knew too much about her already.

Abby stepped inside her home office and went directly to her desk. As she sat down, she saw him still standing at the door and gaping at the room.

"Well, say something."

"I've never seen so much pink in my life."

She saw his gaze drop to the area rug. It was nearly room size and hot pink with pale pink flowers. As he took a few more steps into the room, he looked at the daybed. It was covered with a pale pink throw. The end tables were white and held glass lamps etched with pink roses.

"It was just for me, so I decorated in a way that would remind me that—" She stopped talking and glanced away.

"I know," he said in a surprisingly gentle voice. "Sometimes we need a reminder that we're more than the person we let the world see."

"Yes, exactly." Putting things together and seeing the bigger picture was what he did as a detective, but knowing how easily he could read her was a surprise. "Everyone sees me as a tomboy, always in jeans and, more often than not, covered in hay. But part of me likes girly things—like pink." She shrugged. "That's the side no one sees. Do you have a hidden side, too?"

He nodded but didn't elaborate. "Your computer?" he said, getting back to business.

She typed in several commands, then waved toward the screen. "There you go. That's a new email but it's just like the others."

"How many have you received so far?" he asked.

"Six, maybe eight. I haven't really kept count."

"All by the same sender?" he asked.

"Yeah, 'Crazyman.' He's insisting that I close the ranch before a kid's murdered." She shuddered. "Listen to this one."

Preston leaned over her shoulder as she read Crazyman's latest email out loud.

"'In prison Sinclair was known as Shadowman because no one, not even the law, knew much about his past. His secrets will now haunt you and your ranch. Shut down and get out before someone else dies.'"

Abby swallowed hard. "And look at the top. He sent a copy to the local TV channel. He's trying to destroy this ranch and bury it under a ton of bad publicity, but why?"

"What he doesn't realize is that he's just given us a new lead. Crazyman knows something about Carl Sinclair's past that we didn't—until now. I'm going to do whatever's necessary to find him, but to track him down I'll need a copy of your files."

"No problem. I'll get what you need," she said, reaching for a flash drive. "I hope you catch this creep. I don't care who he is. No one's running me out of here."

"Leaving wouldn't be such a bad idea, Abby, at least temporarily. Take yourself out of danger until we can close this case."

"Do you think I'm not tempted?" She blinked back tears of frustration. "But if I do I'm just another person who can't walk her talk. I tell the kids to hang on and never give up, to believe that things will get better. Yet if I can't stand my ground now, who am I to speak to them of courage? I'll be admitting that fear has the power to derail everything in its path."

Silence stretched out between them.

"That's a good reason to stay," he said at last. "Navajos believe that good is necessary to keep evil in check. As a detective, that's what I try to do—restore the balance. You're doing that, too, by standing up to someone who's trying to bully you."

"It's not an easy choice but I have to make my stand here."

"Then I'll fight beside you," he said. "But think hard about getting surveillance cameras—not for the long run, just for now. They can be hidden from view, or disguised, so no one except you would have to know they're there."

"That all sounds expensive, and our budget's already

strained to the limit. Do you know anyone who might be willing to donate the service, maybe as a tax write-off?"

"As a matter of fact, I do. How about Level One Security?"

Her eyes grew wide. "They're one of the top companies in the state. They even protect government buildings. Do you think there's a chance I could talk them into it?"

"Oh yeah. I know the owner. He's overbearing and a pain in the butt, but deep down—I mean *really* deep down—he's a great guy," he said and grinned. "Daniel Hawk, the owner, is my brother, and another brother of mine and his wife are his partners."

"Great! Then I have the inside track. Can we gang up on Daniel?"

He laughed. "That's the spirit. I'll try to bring him over tomorrow. Okay?"

"Absolutely…and thanks."

"See that? I'm not so bad, even if I'm not wild about pink."

"You're wild enough at the right times." She'd meant it as a mischievous compliment, but his response took her breath away. His eyes darkened instantly and the storm raging there made her weak at the knees.

"I have to get back to the station. I want to drop the flash drive off at the lab so the tech can work on it. He keeps odd hours and I'm betting he's still there."

She led the way back up the hall to the front of the house. "My life here at the ranch has never been easy, but there's no place I'd rather be—even now," she said, standing by the front door.

"Dedication is almost a bad word these days, but not in my book. Nothing worthwhile ever comes easy, Abby." He lingered a moment longer. "But fight the right battles."

His gentleness soothed her even as it made her yearn for more. Yet that side of him vanished the instant he stepped outside.

Preston took in the area with the cold, practiced eye of a cop. "Trust no one, Abby."

"Except you?"

He held her gaze and brushed his roughened palm against the side of her face. "No, not even me."

Chapter Twelve

Preston had gotten practically no sleep last night because he kept thinking about Abby. She was in danger. Every instinct he'd developed over the years as a cop assured him of that.

More than ever, he needed to keep things strictly professional with her. Yet every time he closed his eyes he remembered how soft she'd felt against him and how good she'd tasted.

He glanced at the clock on his nightstand. It was five-thirty. With a curse, he tossed aside the covers and stood. Naked, he parted the curtains and gazed into the woods area behind his house.

He liked being a bachelor and the freedom that came with it. The only neighbors he had here were the wildlife. After several break-ins at his old apartment, he'd purposely bought a place that was hard to find. Here, if someone came after him, he wouldn't endanger anyone else. A cop made enemies. That was just the way it was.

It was also another reason why he had to keep his hands off Abby. She deserved more than he could offer. She was a woman who played for keeps and he wasn't the type to make commitments.

As a homicide cop he faced danger every day. He enjoyed the challenges and risks that came with the job, but some things—like love—were just too big a gamble.

Trusting in those kinds of relationships went against what life had taught him. Everything had two sides, including love. It could satisfy and fulfill for a while, but it also had the power to destroy whatever it touched.

But there was something about Abby that made him want to take a chance. He'd never met anyone like her. Not many people outside his family understood his dedication to law enforcement. Abby not only knew where he was coming from, but she also had a passion of her own to pursue.

He licked his dry lips and for a moment could almost taste her there. He grew hard despite his attempt to hold on to common sense. What the heck was wrong with him? He knew plenty of women who'd be happy with whatever conditions he cared to set. Abby was off-limits.

He stepped into the shower, hoping to cool his blood, and soon discovered that the water heater had shut down sometime during the night. The water was ice cold. Maybe it was an omen. Cursing, he moved fast.

By the time he finished getting dressed, coffee was brewed, thanks to the timer set last night. Dark and strong, just the way he liked it. He took the cup to his desk and checked his work emails. He'd filed his report last night and asked the IT tech to track Abby's emails ASAP. The guy had been working on it when Preston finally left the station. Though he hadn't expected the results this early, the answer was already there in his inbox.

It was six-thirty now. That meant Daniel and Gene, both early risers, would be awake. Kyle, probably not. With a devilish grin, he telephoned Kyle first.

He heard his brother's groggy voice as he answered the call. "What the—"

"It's Preston. I need your special skills."

"Dude, this early?" he growled. "My special skill right now is sleeping. Unless someone's dying, can it wait till, say, nine?"

"No," Preston said. "I need you to go to Señor Java, that coffee shop on West Central. Abby Langdon's been receiving some threatening emails, and I just learned that they originated from that location. The sender used a fake email address and they were sent via Wi-Fi. That's as far as our guys at the station could track it."

"So, why don't you go talk to the staff?"

"No can do. The owner hates cops and knows most of us, but she won't know you. Since there's no last name to connect us, you should be okay, but here's the deal. If the owner finds out you're working with us, she'll bounce you right out on your butt."

"She?" Kyle asked, sounding more interested now.

"Yeah, she. Jade Solis is one hot babe but hard as flint."

"Just the way I like them," Kyle said.

"Since when have you ever been choosy, bro?" Preston said with a laugh. "Just see if you can get me a lead. The last two emails were sent yesterday, one before 8:00 a.m. and the other after 6:00 p.m."

"Like before and after an eight-to-five job. Got it. I'll get what you need and check in with you later."

"Watch yourself."

"She have an in-house boyfriend?"

"Nah, but Jade won a national mixed martial arts competition last year. In high school, she was the only girl on the wrestling team. She doesn't need anyone to back her up. She's the entire package all by herself."

"Glad I have health insurance," he said, laughing. "Guess you're gonna owe me one."

"Just watch your step. I don't want to have to bring you flowers at the hospital."

"Nah, I'm a lover, not a fighter."

Preston hung up and laughed out loud. He'd known this was the kind of assignment Kyle would never turn down.

Next, he called Daniel and explained what he needed. "Sitting Tall Ranch is in bad need of a good security system that includes hidden cameras. It's a short-term thing and it's got to be pro bono."

"I've heard of Abby Langdon's troubles and know what's going on. I've got some surplus equipment just sitting on the shelf that I can configure for her, but first I'll need to look at the layout of her place," Daniel said.

"Don't let anyone know what you're doing. I have a strong suspicion that the perp works there in one capacity or another."

"How soon do you want to move on this?" Daniel asked.

"I can meet you at Sitting Tall Ranch this morning and you can have a look around, but actually putting up cameras will have to wait till no one's there."

"Not a problem. I'll have to check the cameras I have on hand and see which ones meet her needs. Each job requires something different, and I've got several models on hand. So how soon do you want to meet?" Daniel said.

"Thirty-five minutes?"

"We can be there in thirty. I'll bring Gene with me. He stayed over last night. Had some business in town, then a flat tire and by then it was too late to drive back up to his ranch."

"Not buying it, bro. Lori probably kicked his sorry butt out," he joked, knowing from the difference in sound quality that Daniel had put him on speaker.

"Now you're the expert on women?" Gene called out. "Dude, when's the last time you dated a woman long enough to remember her last name?"

"No woman with a brain would put up with him," Daniel said. "After a few hours listening to him talk shop, she'll break out in tears, make up some excuse about her sick friend, then run for the door."

"Nice. Okay, guys, time to go to work—you know, what real men do to earn a living."

"Yeah, yeah," Daniel said. "See you when we get there."

AFTER BEING INTRODUCED to Daniel and Gene, Abby excused herself. "I've got to meet with Stan and crunch some numbers. It won't take long. Walk around and make yourselves at home," she said.

Preston accompanied Daniel, who was taking snapshots and jotting down notes. Gene had gone ahead to check on Big Red.

"She'll need at least two cameras covering her home, two outside in the barn and bunkhouse area and a few special ones inside," Daniel said. "They'll have to work with infrared, too."

As they finished the walk-through, Abby hurried up to them. "Sorry. I'm running behind this morning," she said, "but I sure do appreciate you coming out, Daniel. Any help you can give me will be appreciated."

"The way I see it, you'll need several cameras in key places. Those will relay everything to an off-site location, and if anything looks odd or the system malfunctions the police will be called in immediately."

"That sounds terrific, but I'm not sure it's fair to you. Having people constantly monitoring cameras will run into serious money. Since it's pro bono, maybe you could just put up a couple of cameras and record activity during off hours."

Daniel shook his head. "My tactics are proactive. I don't do things halfway," he said. "You do excellent work and my company's happy to help you out."

Gene arrived just then. "Big Red loves his new home, Abby. Nice to know he's in good hands," he said, then glanced at his brother, a mischievous twinkle in his eye. "Dan's always been slow to join the party, but I'm glad he's found a way to contribute to Sitting Tall Ranch."

Seeing Daniel's eyes narrow as he glared at his brother, she smiled. "I'm very happy to accept whatever help you give us." She fished a set of keys out of her jeans pocket and handed it to Daniel. "These will give you access to every lock on the ranch and to my house. Just return them when you're done installing the cameras…or is that something you turn over to your staff?"

"Usually my people do this, but not this time."

"Thanks so much, Daniel. Now, if you'll excuse me, I have a few more animals waiting for breakfast and water troughs to top off. I'll be back in five or ten minutes."

"I'll help out with the water. Be right back, guys," Preston said, and he smiled at Abby as they walked away.

PRESTON CAME BACK five minutes later, alone. Abby had stopped to groom a mare in a pen about a hundred feet away.

Daniel grinned from ear to ear and Gene patted Preston on the shoulder. "How about that—you two taking care of the animals—together."

"Yup, that's the way it starts. I hope she doesn't break your heart, bro. She's beautiful and sexy. In other words, *way* out of your league," Gene said, watching Abby place a halter on a horse, who obligingly lowered his head for her. "That's a sweet ride."

"Watch your mouth, or I'll close it for you right now," Preston said.

"I was talking about the horse but, hey, if you want to fight, don't worry, I'll take a dive. Don't want you to get beat up in front of your lady," Gene said.

"She's not my lady," Preston said, his voice practically a snarl.

"Enough, guys. Here she comes, and she picked up a guest along the way, and not just the horse. Play nice in front of the kid," Daniel said, cocking his head toward Abby, who was walking toward them with Bobby and the mare on a lead rope between them.

"This is Bobby Neskahi," Abby said a moment later, introducing the boy, then looking at Preston. "He just told me something you need to hear, Preston," she said, then looked at Bobby and nodded. "Go ahead."

"I didn't think of it sooner or I would have said something," Bobby said.

"What is it, son?" Preston asked.

"I told you that Carl didn't have friends here except me and Abby, but I'd forgotten something. Carl had one friend he didn't want anyone to know about—even me. The guy was only here once that I know about. It was in the evening and when Carl saw me coming up the walk to the bunkhouse he almost shoved the guy out the back door. I don't think Carl wanted me to see the guy's face."

"When was this?"

Bobby thought about it. "Before school let out. More than a month ago, I guess."

"What makes you think they were friends?" Preston asked.

"I heard Carl tell him that their days doing time were behind them and they needed to move on. Then he hugged him, like they were buds."

"So, Bobby, you never saw his face?" Preston asked.

"Not then, no, but I went around the bunkhouse and pretended to be petting the llamas. The guy walked right past me like I wasn't even there, just another kid, you know?"

"Bobby, you'll never be 'just' another anything," he said and smiled. "What made you remember now?"

"Abby asked me if I knew a tagger who wore a hoodie because she'd had trouble with one yesterday," Bobby said. "The only person I could think of was Carl's friend. He'd worn a dark blue hoodie, but it wasn't covering his head at the time."

Preston glanced at Abby. "Any objections if I show Bobby some mug shots?"

"It's not my call," Abby said.

"I'll clear it with his foster parents," Preston said.

Preston watched Abby walk off with the boy, and by the time he glanced back at his brothers, both were grinning.

Irritated, Preston glanced away and dialed. Sometimes family could be a real pain in the butt.

Chapter Thirteen

Narrowing down a list of Carl's cellmates didn't take long, and showing their photos to Bobby went even faster.

As his foster mother came inside Abby's office to pick him up, Bobby looked at Preston. "Do you want me to go with you when you pay the guy a visit, just to make sure it's the same person and all that?"

"That's not necessary," Preston said, shaking his head.

"Bobby, you have physical therapy today and we're going. That's the end of it," Kay Yarrow said.

"You heard her," Abby said. "We'll see you tomorrow."

Seeing Bobby look so dejected tugged at Preston. "Can I have a quick word with him before he goes?"

Kay Yarrow nodded.

Preston took the boy into the next room. "I know you want to look out for Abby, so I've got a special job for you. Whenever you're here at the ranch, keep your eyes open and call me if you see anything that doesn't seem right—anything at all, okay?" He handed Bobby his card.

"Seriously?"

Seeing the look of hope in Bobby's eyes reminded Preston of his own past. He knew what Bobby was going through. Until *Hosteen* Silver had come along, he'd lived in one foster home after another—a disposable kid—wanting desperately to belong somewhere and believing it would never happen.

Bobby had made a place for himself here at the ranch and was afraid that it was about to go away, leaving him alone again.

"You love Abby and this ranch, so I can't think of anyone who'd do a better job of keeping an eye on things."

"I would have done it anyway, you know?" Bobby looked up at Preston.

"I know," Preston said. "But it's official now. Get going."

"I hate physical therapy. It never really gets me anywhere, not with stuff that counts. No matter what I do, I'll never be able to play——" He shook his head, then shrugged.

"Play what?"

"It's dumb, I know. I just wish I could play baseball, or at least catch or hit a ball, but I suck. Everyone else just laughs."

"Then let's make a deal. You keep your eyes open, and I'll teach you to catch and hit a baseball."

Preston heard Kay clear her throat. "Time to go now—seriously," he added.

Bobby left with a smile on his face and Abby noticed it immediately. "Those physical therapy sessions are really tough on him. The exercises can be painful, and sometimes it's hard to see progress," she said. "What on earth did you say to cheer him up like that?"

"Just guy talk," he said. "I offered to teach him how to play ball."

"He's been wanting that for a long time. I tried, but I can't pitch or throw, let alone hit a ball. I wasn't much help."

"Then I'll teach both of you," he said. Then he showed her the mug shot of the man Bobby had identified. "Do you know this man?"

Abby studied the photo. "What's his name? He looks vaguely familiar, but I can't place him."

"Edwin Bain," he said.

Abby's forehead furrowed. "It's that scar above his left eyebrow…" After a moment she looked back up at Preston. "I've seen him, but his name isn't Edwin, or even Ed. If I'm right, that's Greg…no wait, Gary something. His hair is lighter and longer, and his face is fuller, too."

"How sure are you that it's the same guy?"

"He looks older now than in that picture, but I'm pretty sure it's him. He calls that his lucky scar," she said, pointing, "because a half inch lower and he might have lost his eye. I must have embarrassed him when I asked about it because the next time I saw him he'd let his hair grow out even more, covering it up."

"And you met him where?"

"Last time I saw him, he was working at Barton's Feed Store."

"Looks like that's where I'm going next."

"Maybe I should go to help point him out. That's an old photo, and the scar's hidden."

He thought about it a few seconds. "Okay, stay behind me. Once you confirm he's the guy you have in mind, I'll take it from there."

Soon they were on their way in Preston's SUV. Abby glanced around. "This fits you."

"What? The SUV?"

"Yeah," she said, and with a tiny grin, added, "It's powerful, stealthy and unmarked."

He took a deep breath. "I'm not unmarked."

"Tattoo?"

He smiled.

"Aw come on—how about a hint, like what and where?"

He remained silent.

"Not even a tiny clue?"

"Nope."

He stared at the road and tried to stay focused, but the light fragrance she wore was making him crazy. It was a gentle scent, like lavender in the spring, and difficult to ignore, just like she was.

"What do you plan to say to Carl's cellmate—if that's him?"

"I need to find out everything he knows about Carl. The murder may be linked to an enemy Carl made back in prison."

"You think someone followed him to the ranch after all these years? Carl served four years and had been out six months before I hired him. That was two years ago."

"Some people have long memories," he said, glancing in the rearview mirror. "Hang on." He made a sharp turn onto a side street without signaling.

"What the—"

"Just checking to see if my hunch was right. A white car was following us. It was staying well back, but it was there."

She turned around in her seat. "Are you sure it's gone?"

"Yeah. It kept going straight."

Preston made several more turns, took an alternate route, then finally pulled up next to Barton's Feed Store and parked. The lot held only three cars at the moment, but the small, locally owned feed store made a slow, steady business.

Because the main building was small, Barton's stored stock tanks and feeders outside behind chain-link fences. Two men were working there, trying to rearrange the pallets to maximize space. The tarps that would be placed over them to protect the merchandise lay nearby on the ground.

"Gary works in the back at the loading dock. He usually helps me load the bales into my truck."

"Let's go there first, then," Preston said.

Knowing ex-cons could spot a cop miles away, Preston forced himself to walk at a leisurely pace. He didn't want Gary, aka Ed, to make a run for it if he was involved.

Once they came around the corner of the building, Abby

spotted the man. "There, on top of that stack of hay bales," she said, pointing.

The man stood about eight feet above them.

"Hey, Miss Langdon," he said, seeing her. "How many bales do you need today?"

"Can you give me a few minutes of your time first?" she asked. As he started to come down, Abby added, "My friend would like to ask you some questions."

He was halfway down the stack when he saw Preston standing there, looking up.

"I'm Detective Bowman. Relax. I just have a few questions for you."

Gary kicked at a bale of hay, knocking it off the stack and down toward Preston, then tried to slide off the back of the pile.

Preston, who'd managed to jump aside just in time, ducked around and grabbed Gary's leg before he reached the ground.

Gary tried to twist free but fell on his back from three bales up. Preston pinned the man in place with his knee, twisting his arm behind his back to keep him there.

"You've got no right—" Gary said.

"Buddy, you just assaulted a police officer."

"I stepped wrong on a bale of hay while climbing down, lost my balance and the bale fell next to you. It was an accident."

"Tell that to your parole officer."

"Look, I freaked out when you said 'detective.' Cut me some slack, will you? It took me four months to find this job."

Preston jerked the guy to his feet.

"What's going on?" a man's voice suddenly boomed behind them.

"Mr. Barton, it's okay," Gary said. "One of the bales slipped off the stack, that's all. I was apologizing for the accident."

Tim Barton glanced at Preston, noting the badge on his belt. "Is that what happened, Officer?"

"There's no problem here," Preston said. "I only need to ask your employee some questions about a friend of his. It won't take long."

Barton looked at Abby. "Word's out about what happened at the ranch. Now I hear parents are afraid to let their kids volunteer there until the killer's caught. I think you're getting a raw deal, so the next fifty bales are on me."

"Thanks!" Abby went up to Barton. "Let's go back inside. I need to place an order."

"Can you use a few bags of grain, too?"

"Yes, that would be terrific!" she said and walked off with the owner.

Preston bit back a smile. There was just something about Abby and her dream that brought out the best in people.

He looked back at Gary—Ed Bain—his expression turning hard. Good, for some reason, also attracted evil. "If you know something, you might as well spill it now. Your job may be hanging in the balance."

"I went to visit Carl after I got paroled. I was hoping he would talk to the ranch's owner and help me land a job, but he wouldn't even hear me out. He had a good thing going and didn't want to screw it up, I guess."

"Tell me about Carl. What was he into? Drugs, something else?"

"Carl? You've got to be kidding. The only thing he was really into was art, and these days he was perfectly happy doing his own charcoal sketches. He was good, too. When I first heard that he got offed, I figured he'd gotten himself involved with some art dealer who wanted him to forge some drawings for him."

"Did you have a solid reason to believe that?" Preston asked.

"Just what I knew about him. He was always sketching, doing stuff that was usually better than what you'd see in art galleries. I once asked him why he didn't put some of his work up on the internet and make a few extra bucks, but he said he wasn't interested. Maybe he was trying to avoid the attention. I always had the feeling that he was hiding from someone or something, and that's why he was living under the radar—no phone, no car, no nothing," he said. "That's all I know."

"If you think of anything else, call me," Preston said and handed him his card. "And don't leave town."

Preston walked across the yard and saw a face he recognized: Marsha Robertson, the TV reporter. She was sitting inside her white sedan and looking directly at him.

Preston walked over and leaned in the driver's side. "What brings you here?"

"Probably the same thing as you. Looking for leads into Carl Sinclair's death and trying to find out how it all ties in to the ranch."

"There is no tie to the ranch other than the crime happened there." He stood up straight. "You were following me before. Don't do it again. If you do, I'll arrest you for interfering with an ongoing police investigation. Clear?"

"You win this round, Detective Bowman."

Preston stood back as Marsha drove off. Moments later, Abby came up. "Was that the reporter?"

"Yeah, she was the one who was tailing us. I tried to warn her off," he said, then shrugged. "It won't do any good though. She's after a story, so nothing I say is really going to make her back away."

"I'll deal with whatever trouble she creates as it happens. Right now I really should get back to the ranch."

"Has something happened?"

"I want to talk to Bobby. The Yarrows are planning to take all the boys up to their cabin in the mountains this coming weekend, but Bobby hates it there. He wants permission to stay at the ranch until they return," she said. "Bobby has a tough time because he can't go hiking without slowing everyone down, and that creates problems with the other boys. They give him a hard time. Bobby always ends up being left behind."

"You're going to let him stay?"

She nodded. "I told Kay I'd put him up, and do everything I can to make sure he's safe. He'll help with the animals and there's always room—and a need for an extra pair of hands willing to work."

"And you like having him around."

She nodded and smiled. "Yeah, I do. I love Bobby. He's a great kid."

"He'd do just about anything for you."

"That's exactly the same way I feel about him."

"Have you ever considered fostering him?" Preston asked. In his day, strangers would often invite foster kids to their homes for special events, like holiday parties. Things had changed a lot in the past twenty years, but people still drew the line when it came to getting involved full-time. They had lives of their own.

"There are a lot of rules when it comes to fostering, and they're there for good reasons," she said. "The truth is, Bobby needs more than I can give him. Unlike the dad he barely knew, Bobby needs a male role model who'll see him as differently abled, as opposed to disabled."

"I hear you," he said with a thoughtful nod. "I've never been physically challenged, but I know how tough things can be for disposable kids."

"*Disposable* kids?" she asked, looking at him in surprise as they got into the SUV.

"That's what we called ourselves back then." He saw the look of sympathy in her eyes and turned away. He'd hated it back then and it was no different now. "It was a way of reminding ourselves that we had to learn to deal."

"How did you end up in foster care, Preston?" she asked softly. "Do you mind if I ask?"

Silence stretched between them as Preston drove toward the ranch. His situation wasn't exactly a secret. He'd give her the facts and let it go at that. "My mom had an issue with drugs. One day she didn't come home. I had a cleaning job at the hardware store, so I had enough cash to get by for a while. After a month, social workers showed up on my doorstep and I was placed in a foster home," he said, his tone letting her know that he didn't need, nor want, sympathy.

She got the message and offered neither.

"I think what bothers Bobby most is that, although it's a tribe-approved home, he's the only Navajo there right now. Child Services is trying to find him a Navajo family, but only a limited number of foster homes are licensed by the tribe. Since Bobby needs specialized care that's more readily available here in Hartley, they've kept him with the Yarrows. It's a good compromise, but he's had problems getting along with the other kids."

"I remember my first foster home. I was the only Navajo there, too, and I took some grief, but each one of those kids was hurting. Most of them believed they hadn't measured up somehow, and that's why they'd been placed in the system. Others coped by convincing themselves that their parents would be back for them soon. Bobby's story about his father being a spy is more imaginative than most, but it's not unusual."

"Did you make up a story for yourself?"

"No. I knew my mother wouldn't be coming back. She had other…priorities."

"How old were you?"

"Twelve."

Abby reached for his hand. "What she did made you a stronger man. I can't imagine anyone I'd like in my corner more than you."

Her words took him by surprise. Most people offered pity. Yet the way Abby was looking at him made him feel invincible, like one of the legendary warriors of his tribe.

"I'm sure that Bobby senses that you two are alike in some ways. That's why he trusts you," she said.

He shook his head. "No, I don't think it's trust. Bobby sees me as a necessary evil. If he cooperates with me, maybe I can solve the case a little faster. Then things will get back to normal for you and him. With Bobby, trust has to be earned."

"Is that the way it is with you?"

"Yeah. In that way I'm no different than Bobby."

He remembered the bad times like they were yesterday. When a person who's supposed to love you no matter what bails, everything changes. The hurt fades eventually, but distrust remains, a scar that'll always be there.

As they pulled up in front of the ranch, Abby asked Preston to stop by the mailbox. After retrieving her mail, she hopped back into the SUV.

"Thanks. You saved me having to walk back," she said, then suddenly stopped sorting through the stack.

"Is something wrong?" he asked.

"This letter has no stamp on it," she said, holding it up for him to see. "I'm hoping it's a donation. Sometimes people will leave a check, or cash, for us in the mailbox." She tore open the envelope, then stiffened.

"It's not a donation," she said in a taut voice. "This is from the same person who's been emailing me."

"Crazyman?"

"Yeah. He wants Sitting Tall Ranch closed for good."

FREE Merchandise is 'in the Cards' for you!

Dear Reader,

We're giving away FREE MERCHANDISE!

Seriously, we'd like to reward you for reading this novel by giving you **FREE MERCHANDISE** worth over **$20**. And no purchase is necessary!

You see the Jack of Hearts sticker above? Paste that sticker in the box on the Free Merchandise Voucher inside. Return the Voucher promptly...and we'll send you valuable Free Merchandise!

Thanks again for reading one of our novels—and enjoy your Free Merchandise with our compliments!

Pam Powers

Pam Powers

P.S. Look inside to see what Free Merchandise is **"in the cards"** for you!

W
e'd like to send you two free books to introduce you to the Harlequin Intrigue® series. These books are worth over $10, but they are yours to keep absolutely FREE! We'll even send you 2 wonderful surprise gifts. You can't lose!

REMEMBER: Your Free Merchandise, consisting of **2 Free Books** and **2 Free Gifts**, is worth over $20.00! No purchase is necessary, so please send for your Free Merchandise today.

Plus TWO FREE GIFTS!

We'll also send you two wonderful FREE GIFTS (worth about $10), in addition to your 2 Free Harlequin Intrigue books!

Visit us at:
www.ReaderService.com

YOUR FREE MERCHANDISE INCLUDES...

2 FREE Harlequin Intrigue® Books

AND 2 FREE Mystery Gifts

FREE MERCHANDISE VOUCHER

2 FREE
BOOKS
and
2 FREE
GIFTS

Please send my Free Merchandise, consisting of
2 Free Books and **2 Free Mystery Gifts**.
I understand that I am under no obligation to buy
anything, as explained on the back of this card.

❏ I prefer the regular-print edition   ❏ I prefer the larger-print edition
182/382 HDL F4ZP   199/399 HDL F4ZP

Please Print

FIRST NAME

LAST NAME

ADDRESS

APT.#   CITY

STATE/PROV.   ZIP/POSTAL CODE

Offer limited to one per household and not applicable to series that subscriber is currently receiving.
Your Privacy—The Harlequin® Reader Service is committed to protecting your privacy. Our Privacy Policy is available
online at www.ReaderService.com or upon request from the Harlequin Reader Service. We make a portion of our mailing
list available to reputable third parties that offer products we believe may interest you. If you prefer that we not exchange
your name with third parties, or if you wish to clarify or modify your communication preferences, please visit us at
www.ReaderService.com/consumerchoice or write to us at Harlequin Reader Service Preference Service, P.O. Box 9062,
Buffalo, NY 14269. Include your complete name and address.

NO PURCHASE NECESSARY!

Chapter Fourteen

She couldn't keep her hands from shaking, so Abby kept the letter on her lap as she read it out loud. "'Your first mistake brought death. How many more will pay if you keep the ranch open?'"

Her voice wavered on the last line and she swallowed hard.

"Don't let him get to you. That's what he wants."

"I'm responsible for hiring Carl, and if you're right, danger followed him here. Am I now endangering everyone else connected to the ranch just so I can keep things going?"

"There's no reason to believe that, and you're already taking all the precautions you can. Except for Bobby, who you're keeping close, you don't have kids coming in right now. You're only doing what has to be done, like taking care of the livestock."

"I trusted Carl, and look what's happened. If I'm that bad a judge of character, maybe I'm not fit to run the ranch," she whispered, voicing her greatest fear.

Though her voice had been barely audible, he still managed to hear her.

"You're letting him twist your thinking," he said. "I'll tell you what. Let's get down to basics. You trust me, right?"

"Of course."

"See that? You're an excellent judge of character," he said. She smiled.

As Preston parked in front of the ranch's office, Abby saw Bobby standing on the sidewalk, waiting. "I have to know whether Carl was doing anything illegal here, Preston. For my own sake and that of the ranch."

"I'll find out," he said. "Right now I'd like to talk to some of your volunteers. I see a few faces I haven't spoken to before."

"Some of the younger kids have flexible schedules that depend on whether they've got exams or other school activities. During the summer, they pretty much come and go all the time. A handful of our adults are also on drop-by status. It sounds a little crazy, but everything gets done."

"All right. Looks like we've each got work to do," he said, gesturing toward Bobby.

"Feel free to talk to anyone you want and wander around. I'm going to see what's up with Bobby," Abby said and picked up the mail.

"Leave the one from Crazyman in the SUV. The chances of getting prints from it are remote, but you never know."

As Preston walked off, Abby went to meet Bobby. She had the mail clutched so tightly in her hand she bent the edges, a detail Bobby didn't miss.

He shot Preston a dirty look.

Catching it, Abby eased her grip and forced herself to smile. "Bobby, you're back early. Something wrong?"

"No, PT was cancelled. Air-conditioning went out. Looks like you're the person with something wrong," he added.

"What do you mean?" Abby saw that Bobby was watching Preston, who was out of earshot.

"He said he could help, but he hasn't. That's why something's bothering you. Right?"

"I got some bad news, but it has nothing to do with Preston. He's doing his best."

"Wait—he wants you to call him by his first name? It's a trick," he added quickly. "They only make friends with you when they want something. That's what happened last year when one of my foster brothers got arrested. The cop was real nice to us, then he came to get Rodney."

Abby sighed. Bobby wasn't a normal ten-year-old, but it saddened her to see just how cynical he'd become already. "Detective Bowman's not like that."

"You *like* him?"

"Yes, of course. He's working hard to find answers, and when he does, I can open up the ranch again."

"Yeah—but you *like* him?" he asked, giving the word a deeper meaning by emphasizing it.

"Maybe," she said, understanding what he meant. "I really don't know him all that well yet."

"He likes you."

"What makes you say that?" she asked, curious.

"I see the way he looks at you."

She laughed. "He looks at me when he talks to me. So do most people, Bobby."

He shook his head. "No. When you're *not* looking. He likes you," he repeated.

"Bobby, you're imagining things. Now let's get to work. We need to groom the camels, and you're good with Hank. You can get him to *koosh,* to lie down, so we can reach his back."

Bobby smiled. "I like Hank."

"Yeah, I know. He likes you, too. I don't let just anyone groom him, you know."

Bobby practically beamed. As they walked, he looked away from her and in a whisper, said, "I like the detective, too."

"Was it that hard to admit?"

He shrugged. "He said he'd teach me to play ball. I hope he keeps his word."

"Wait and see, then you'll know."

After they'd brushed Hank, Abby saw Preston trying to

talk to one of her volunteers, a college-aged girl. She kept turning her back on him as she worked.

"Looks like the detective needs my help," Bobby said.

"He does, does he?" Abby replied with a tiny smile.

"Yeah, he's not getting anywhere. Cassie won't even look at him. He's making her nervous. If I go with him, maybe people won't feel like he's about to arrest them or something."

"Maybe so, but you should probably ask him if he wants your help first. If he says not now, then come back."

"Okay."

As Bobby walked off, she saw Ilse Sheridan leading Big Red into one of the big enclosures. Abby went to meet her.

"You're early today. Thanks for giving us some extra time, Ilse."

"Glad to help out. Rod wanted me to drop off some donations he got for you from his NBA buddies. With the new rumor that's going around, he was afraid donors would be few and far between, at least for a while."

"I don't understand. What rumor?"

"You haven't heard?" Ilse stared at her in surprise. "It's just gossip, but it'll have an effect."

"Go on," Abby said.

"Some people are saying you need to be audited to prove that donations are really going to the ranch. Carl was a convicted thief, so they're wondering what else was going on here."

She felt the blood drain from her face, but dismay soon turned to anger. "That's beneath contempt. My finances are an open book." Seeing Stan by the ranch's office door, Abby waved, signaling him to wait for her. "I'm going to stop that nonsense in its tracks."

PRESTON SAW ABBY storm away from Ilse Sheridan. Curious, he figured he'd go talk to Ilse next. Officers Jerry Michaels and Gabe Sanchez had collected statements from those present the day Carl's body had been found. Now he needed to account for the whereabouts of the rest of the workers here and see if they had an alibi that covered the vic's time of death.

As he approached Ilse, Preston caught a glimpse of Bobby out of the corner of his eye. The kid was hanging back, but Preston knew he was listening to everything that was going on.

"Ilse Sheridan?" he said. "Remember me?"

"Detective Bowman," she said with a nod. "How may I help you?"

"I'd like you to answer a few questions for me."

"I'd be happy to," she said.

"Do you normally volunteer here this time of day?"

She shook her head. "No, not usually. I made an exception today because Mr. Garner asked me to come by and drop off some donations he'd collected on behalf of the ranch."

"Where were you last Sunday between nine and midnight?"

"You don't honestly think I had—"

Preston held up one hand. "I'm asking everyone the same question. It's just procedure."

Ilse relaxed. "I came after work and stayed till around ten, maybe a bit after. I was exercising Tracker. I take him out for a run, then groom him and put him away for the night."

"Who else was still here when you left?"

She paused, considering it for several long moments. "That's hard to say for sure because this place is so big. Usually though, by ten everyone's gone. Abby gets up real early, too, so sometimes she's already gone to bed by that time. Offhand, I don't remember if her light was on or off when I left that night."

He noted the way Ilse kept glancing to her right, losing eye contact each time she spoke. Instinct and experience told him she was lying or uncomfortable about something.

He continued his questions but soon realized he wasn't getting anywhere. After he thanked her and moved on, Bobby came up to him.

"She didn't tell you everything. Remember when I told you I hear and see things 'cause people don't pay attention to me?" Seeing Preston nod, he continued. "Sometimes Ilse meets Monroe here. They like each other."

"You think they're trying to keep it a secret?"

"Yeah, 'cause when people are around, they barely speak to each other. I know what's going on because I saw them ducking into the toolshed Sunday night. I was still here because my foster dad was late picking me up. He had an extra job. Anyway, I went to the barn to give Tracker some carrots, heard some weird noises and looked through one of the gaps in the wall between the boards. They were in there, kissing and stuff. It was embarrassing."

"Did they see you?"

"Nah. They were too busy with each other. Besides, spies know how to sneak around. I've been practicing. I read what to do in Angus McAdams's book, *Spycraft*. I even bought my own copy."

"How long were you here last Sunday?"

"I left at about seven-thirty or eight."

Preston checked his notes. According to the statement he'd given Gabe Sanchez, Monroe had supposedly been at an Isotopes game in Albuquerque at that time. "You sure you saw them Sunday?"

"Yeah, the next morning...that's when I found Carl," he said in a whisper-thin voice.

Preston considered what he'd just learned. It was possible Ilse and Monroe had been here and maybe seen the killer or knew something they were leaving out to cover their relationship. The Isotopes story could have been a hasty attempt to give the police an unverifiable alibi.

"You think they did it," Bobby said.

It hadn't been a question and that surprised Preston. No one, not even his foster brothers, had ever been able to read him so easily.

"It doesn't matter what I think. I need evidence. Police work isn't about guessing—it's about facts," he said.

"Yeah, I suppose," Bobby said. "Do you think you can hurry up and work faster? This place is all Abby's got, and she's really worried she might lose it."

"I know."

"It can really hurt when you have something really important, then it's taken away, especially when it's not your fault."

Preston felt the tug in his gut. "Yeah. I learned that back when I was in foster care."

Bobby's eyes grew wider. "You were a foster kid? Why'd you become a cop?"

Preston laughed. "Okay, kid, you're going to have to explain that."

"Cops pretend to be your friend, then once they get what they want you never see them again."

Preston walked beside him, trying to figure out what had happened to Bobby. "Not all cops are like that, but it's a tough job. Sometimes it can make the rest of your life…difficult."

Bobby looked at Preston, then back down at the ground. "It's hard to believe anyone when all you get is excuses."

"Yeah, but here's something you can count on from me— I'm going to teach you to play ball."

"I'm not athletic—and it's not just 'cause I've got JRA. I can't catch even when the ball hits me in the hands."

"It's just a matter of timing and practice. I can teach you. And as far as throwing the ball goes, I taught my brother Rick, and that guy couldn't hit the side of a barn when we first started," he said and laughed.

"Did he have problems getting around?"

"Not like yours, but he was a total train wreck. He couldn't go through the house without knocking something over. He was clumsy and overweight back in high school. Now, he's six foot four and trimmed down to around two-twenty."

"Is he still clumsy?"

"That depends on who you ask," Preston said and smiled. He wished he could tell Bobby more about his brother. None of them, except Daniel who'd found out by accident, knew exactly what Rick did for the FBI. Some sort of undercover work—that's all he'd been able to put together. Rick would be home in another year, and Preston was looking forward to seeing him then.

Before Preston could say anything else, he heard tires on gravel and saw a truck pull to a dusty stop by the office. Ed Bain, from the feed store, got out and strode toward Abby.

Sensing trouble, Preston broke into a jog.

"This is your fault, you witch," Bain yelled, raising a fist as he closed in on her.

Preston stepped between them, blocking the man's advance. "Put your hands down."

Bain stopped, lowered his fists, then kicked out, aiming for Preston's groin.

Preston stepped sideways, dodging the kick, then grabbed the man's boot, twisting it like a corkscrew. The man yelled in agony, falling to the ground on his face.

Preston dropped down and grabbed Bain's arm, twisting his hand up toward his neck painfully.

Bain yelped, groping with his other hand to break the hold. Preston just applied more force, and Bain curled up, tears in his eyes.

"Stop resisting," Preston ordered.

Bain gave up, and Preston brought both of the man's wrists together and handcuffed him.

Still holding Bain's arm, Preston looked over at Abby. "You okay?"

"I'm fine," she managed to say in a shaky voice.

"You might as well call my parole officer," Bain spat out. "At least in prison I won't have to beg for food and a place to sleep."

"You have a job. What's your problem?" Abby asked him.

"The problem is you got me fired, you dumb—"

Preston tightened his grip. "Watch your mouth."

"Maybe you should bring him inside," Abby said, noting that all the volunteers were watching.

Preston read him his rights as he pushed him inside Abby's office.

"Yeah, yeah, I've heard it all before. Go ahead and take me in. The job at the feed store was all I could get around here. Now that it's history, so am I."

"Why were you fired?" Abby asked.

"After you left, I managed to smooth things with Barton, but then that reporter came back and started pushing me for answers about Carl. Barton said he didn't need that kind of publicity, so he fired me," Ed said.

"You're talking about Marsha Robertson?" Preston asked him.

"I don't know her name. She's the hot blonde on local TV. She said there's a burglary ring that has been breaking into area houses and she wanted to know if I knew anything about that. She also kept asking about Carl and what had happened between us. She then asked me 'why,' not 'if,' I'd killed Carl. That's the part Barton heard."

"Answer one question for me," Preston said. "Have you been sending Abby Langdon threatening letters? You might as well come clean. You're going to jail anyway."

"Letters? What the hell you talking about now?"

"The person who wrote these letters knew Carl's nickname—Shadowman."

"Dude, everyone in the pen knows each other by their nicknames, and it wasn't just me and him in there." He turned to Abby. "Do I look like the letter-writing type? When I have something to say, I get in your face."

Abby looked at him, then expelled her breath in a soft hiss. "Preston, let him go. He didn't actually hit me and I'm not going to press charges."

"You should," Preston said firmly.

"No. He wouldn't have lost his job if we hadn't led the reporter to him," she said and looked at Ed. "I'm going to ask Tim Barton to take you back."

"If he doesn't, can I work here? I'll do whatever you need. I know animals. Carl and I worked on the same program."

Abby shook his head. "I can't hire you, at least not now. This ranch is under siege. I'm fighting just to keep the animals and pay my bills," she said, "but give me a chance to talk to Tim. I think I can convince him if you agree not to lose your temper again—with anyone."

Seeing him nod, she stepped into the next room while Preston remained with Ed.

"She's not going to press charges. How about you?" Ed asked.

Preston pushed him against the wall and held him there. "If you *ever* lay a hand on her, it will be the last thing you ever do. You get me?"

"I didn't actually do—" Seeing the lethal glare Preston gave him, he stopped speaking and just nodded.

Ten minutes later Abby came back to the room. "Okay, you have your job back but if you give Tim any trouble—being late to work, not doing what you're told, arguing with a customer—you're out."

"I won't give him a reason," he said.

"Remember what I said." Preston's voice was barely a whisper as he removed the man's handcuffs.

Once Ed left, Preston glanced back at Abby. She was looking out the window, her arms wrapped tightly around herself.

He'd never been impulsive, but this time something snapped inside him and he pulled her into his arms. "You're not in this alone, Abby. Your fight is my fight, too."

"No one's ever jumped in for me like that. I should have said thanks…."

The gentleness in her gaze, and the fear that lay beyond that, were too much for him. She needed tenderness, but when he lowered his mouth to hers and her lips flowered open, heat shot through him. His heart began to thunder and heat poured into his veins. She was sweet and soft, the very qualities that were missing from his world of cold, hard facts and logic.

He was demanding and rough, but she surrendered to him easily, giving as much as he wanted to take. Fire coursed through him as he ravaged her mouth. He'd never felt this greed—this overpowering need for someone else.

Yet what raged inside him was more than passion. The proof was there when he moved away from her. "Abby…."

Those big, beautiful hazel eyes stayed on him until he couldn't stand it anymore. "I have to go work on the case. I'll be in touch later."

He strode outside to his SUV, his body aching, his blood on fire. Cursing himself, he got behind the wheel. To help Abby, he'd have to keep his priorities straight and focus on the investigation.

As he tried to get the memory of their kiss out of his mind, he remembered the way she'd looked at him. The longing in her eyes would haunt his dreams long after tonight.

Chapter Fifteen

Preston loved police work. It was at the heart of everything he was and had ever wanted to be. Yet sometimes it was necessary to cut a few corners.

"Call Daniel," he said to the cell phone resting beside him on the seat of his SUV.

"Hey, bro," Daniel greeted over the speaker. "What's going on?"

"I'd like you to get me everything you can on Ilse Sheridan, Stanley Cooper, Michelle Okerman and Monroe Jenkins, my boss's son," he said. Due to his government security contracts Daniel had high-level clearance and could get into databases that would take him a folder of paperwork to access. "I need you to keep it off the record, too."

"Don't I always?"

"One more thing. I want you to see what you can get me on a ward of the state, a child named Robert or Bobby Neskahi. I want to find out about his parents."

"That's a lot tougher. Most of those files are sealed by the Office of Children, Youth and Families or the courts. Are you stopping by later?"

"Yeah. I'm hoping together we can find some answers. Someone's working real hard to close down Sitting Tall Ranch, and I need to find out how it all connects to the murder."

"What are your instincts telling you, bro?"

"That there's way more to this case than I'm seeing, and Sitting Tall Ranch is right in the middle of everything."

PRESTON DROVE TO Stan Cooper's office next. He'd wanted to talk to the accountant away from the ranch. In his own office, the man would be more relaxed and focused, something that would work to Preston's advantage.

He found the place quickly and went inside. While Stan finished a conference call, his leggy blonde assistant offered him a cup of coffee. She was easy on the eyes and flashy but not his type. More like Rick's or Kyle's. Of course, any female was Kyle's type. He smiled at the thought.

Several moments later, he was ushered into the small but well-appointed office. Several black-and-white charcoal sketches hung on the wall, all depicting southwest landscapes and animals. Old black-and-white panoramic photos of Navajo Dam dating back to the sixties were there, too.

"I like the photos," Preston said.

"I spent a lot of my time up in that area as a kid," Stan said, shaking Preston's hand. "So what brings you here, Detective?" he asked, a worried frown on his face.

"I'm digging hard into the case. Since you play a big part at the ranch as accountant, advisor and volunteer, I thought you'd be able to answer a few questions for me."

"That'll depend on the questions," he said. "I can't give you current specifics of Abby's financial situation, but the ranch is a nonprofit so some of those records are public."

Preston took a seat and leaned back in the chair. It was soft leather and probably cost a small fortune, but it was definitely comfortable. "My primary interest is Carl Sinclair's murder."

"Terrible business," Stan said, sitting behind his desk. "Is there a chance it was a random thing? Someone got caught trespassing and Carl stepped in?"

"It's too soon for me to come to any conclusions," Preston

said. "I came looking for your take on the people who work
and volunteer at the ranch. I'd ask Abby, but she tends to see
the best in everyone…"

"And that clouds reality," he said, finishing Preston's un-
spoken thought. "Don't think I haven't spoken to her about
that, but Abby's…well, Abby. She does things her way, and
her idealism sometimes trumps her common sense."

"You see things more objectively, so keeping that in mind,
let's start with Ilse Sheridan and Monroe Jenkins."

He barked a laugh. "You heard about that, did you?" He
shrugged dismissively. "Ilse's only playing with him. In my
opinion she enjoys the attention of a man fifteen years younger
than she is. The fact the kid's the police chief's son just adds
spice to the mix. There's nothing serious going on there, but
you might not want to tell that to Monroe."

"I understand Ilse and Monroe were both close to Carl."
He knew no such thing, but sometimes it helped to intimate
that he knew more than he did. People tended to speak more
freely then.

Stan looked puzzled for a minute, then smiled. "Wait—
you're talking about the nights Monroe and Carl got together
to play chess? Ilse wasn't involved in that. Carl had been de-
pressed about something and Monroe picked up on it. Since
he knew Carl liked chess, he decided to bring a board and
talk him into playing a few games."

"Did it help?"

"I don't know. Carl was hard to read. The guy was a mass
of contradictions, too. He never had much to say and he never
asked anyone for help, but if you needed his, he was always
there to lend a hand. Let me give you an example. Monroe
was having problems at school, and his dad was all over his
case. When Carl found out, he helped Monroe study for his
tests, and the kid passed with flying colors. Carl also helped
me." He rolled up his sleeve to show Preston his silver-and-

turquoise watch. "I love this thing. It was given to me by my father. One day at the ranch, I lost it. We searched everywhere. Nada. Zip. I figured it was gone for good."

"You wear that to the ranch?" Preston asked, eyebrows raised.

"Not usually, no, but that day I was in a hurry and forgot. The catch must have caught on something, and it came off. I was really pissed at myself and tried not to think about it," he said. "The next morning, Carl called. He'd found it down between two bales of hay where I'd been working. I offered Carl a reward, but he wouldn't hear of it."

"He could have easily sold that watch and no one would have been the wiser," Preston said, thinking out loud.

"Yeah, which is why I wanted you to hear about that. Carl was a complicated man. I can't say I trusted him completely, but I think he really appreciated the chance Abby gave him. In my opinion, he wouldn't have willingly messed that up for the world."

Preston took notes, then looked up. "As a businessman, what's your opinion about the ranch's financial situation? Can Sitting Tall Ranch weather the hard times ahead?"

Stan leaned back in his leather chair, a grim look on his face. "It's going to be hard for Abby to keep things running considering her current cash flow problems, but she has an option. If she wants out, I can always make some things happen for her."

"What do you mean?"

"I'm part of an area investment group and we've made her a good offer for the ranch. She stands to make a profit and though it won't be substantial, she'd have enough to relocate to another, smaller ranch."

"What did she say about that?" Preston asked.

"She refused to even consider the deal. She doesn't want to start over. To her, Sitting Tall Ranch is in the perfect location and she's determined to stay and fight, though I've warned her that she could end up losing everything. There's more working against her than the current criminal investigation."

"Like what?"

"My investment group is small but well connected, and although this is nothing but rumor at this point, word reached us that there's a large corporation interested in the land next to her ranch."

"What kind of corporation?" Preston asked.

"J&R Sports Paradise. Attorneys connected to them have been checking zoning requirements, asking for copies of traffic studies and checking utility services. I understand that they want to build one of their full-scale franchises here. That'll include an indoor and outdoor gun range, archery and even a motocross. All that activity next door to the ranch is bound to make the animals less stable and the parents of high-risk kids extremely nervous."

"So what was your investment group planning to do with Abby's land?"

"We've studied that company and know how it works. Once it buys the primary property, it'll target adjacent ones. Then the company will acquire allies in the local government and business community with the promise of more jobs and tax revenues, then move to rezone and even devalue adjacent properties. Our investment group can make sure we're in position to sell at the best possible price before politics force our hand."

"Abby can do the same."

"No, she doesn't have the resources to play that game. Closing this ranch and opening a new one is an expensive proposition. First, she'll have to find a suitable property, then there's the logistics of zoning, obtaining exotic animal permits and finding new donors. She'd also have the cost of housing the animals until she finds a new place. She could sell them, but it took her years to find the right ones. They're all temperament tested and were donations from patrons who wouldn't necessarily be there next time."

"Those are valid concerns. I can see why she'd prefer to fight it out here," Preston said.

"Personally, I think her reluctance goes deeper than that. To her, it's personal, not just business. She's put her heart into that ranch and can't bear the thought of walking away."

Preston exhaled softly. He wondered what part Bobby played in that. She loved that boy, and if she moved, she'd have to leave him behind.

"Thanks for your time, Stan," Preston said, standing up.

Preston left the office and drove directly to Daniel's place. His primary job was to find the killer, and it was possible this other threat to the ranch might have played a role in what had happened. He needed more information.

Preston arrived at Daniel's office on Hartley's west side forty minutes later. He stopped at the gate and seconds later was buzzed in.

Daniel's office was a large rectangular warehouse in the middle of a three-acre compound enclosed by a tall chain-link fence.

Daniel greeted him at the door of the main building. "Figured you'd show up around lunch, so I bought extra. Kyle's eyeing your plate now, so you better hurry."

Preston took a whiff as he stepped inside. "Mrs. Pinto's Navajo Tacos." As he entered the kitchen area of the big, open room, he saw Kyle lifting the lid on the only take-out dish that was still untouched. "Hands off, or I'll have to shoot you."

Kyle laughed. "Can't blame a guy for trying."

As Preston sat down, he glanced over at Daniel. "Anything yet on the background search?"

"Grab your plate and let's get to work," he said, leading the way to the main computer area. They pulled up chairs around the big, table-size flat monitor.

Sweeping his fingers across the display, Daniel transferred the information onto a large, split screen, wall-mounted monitor.

"So far they're all coming out clean. Ilse Sheridan has an MBA from State. She started out at an Ivy League school, but transferred after disciplinary issues that weren't specified. She's worked for Garner for three years, ever since he retired. Near as I can figure, she has no life. She relocates every time he buys a new house—his last one was in Santa Fe. Monroe Jenkins lives at home and is going to community college. Basically he's a B student and clean. So no dirt on the chief's son."

Preston nodded and swallowed his frustration along with a big helping of cheese, meat and tortilla.

"Since I couldn't find much on the other names, I decided to dig deeper into Carl Sinclair's past," Daniel said, removing the previous images and displaying Carl's prison photo and criminal record. "I even called in a favor or two and got one of the correction officers to give me some background. He said that at one point, the head of one of the prison gangs, a bad dude by the name of John Dietz, lost his good luck charm. He assumed someone had stolen it and ended up putting a few inmates in the prison infirmary. As it turned out Dietz had left it in his pants pocket. Carl, on laundry duty, found it and returned it to him. Carl was under Dietz's protection after that. No one messed with him."

"Sounds like Carl had some survival skills," Preston said.

"In prison, yeah, but he lasted less than three years after his release," Kyle said.

"Maybe I need to focus on his career as a thief. According to the reports I've read, everything said to have been stolen by him was eventually recovered, but there's another possibility I haven't been able to check out," Preston said. "What if Carl took paintings that were never reported missing because the victims of those thefts didn't have legal ownership?"

"Unreported crimes? Black market stuff? That's an interesting angle, but it sounds almost impossible to follow up on," Daniel said.

"Yeah, I know." Preston glanced at Kyle. "So what did you get from Jade at the coffee bar? Anything?"

"Well, I got her to talk to me, but I don't have anything you can use. She remembers a guy who comes in early in the morning and after work to sip coffee and use the Wi-Fi, but she said that's her busiest time of day. All she could tell me about him is that he's my size and wears a baseball cap low on his head and shades."

"Inside?" Preston asked.

"Yeah, I asked her that same question. She says that her paying customers can wear whatever they want. If they cause trouble, she takes care of it. Otherwise, as long as they place an order and mind their own business, she leaves them alone," Kyle said. "I'm having dinner with her tonight, so I'll let you know if she remembered anything else."

"You're having dinner with Jade?" Preston asked, surprised.

"Yeah."

Preston expelled his breath in a hiss, then turned his attention back to Dan. "Now I've got to figure out if Carl was somehow involved in the rash of burglaries we've been having all over town."

Daniel shook his head. "No chance. I've already checked into that for you. The nights the last two break-ins took place, Carl was at a fundraiser at the casino that showcased the camels. Celebrity and corporate bigwigs were offered a camel ride into the desert at one grand a pop. They raised twenty thousand that night, but that included a huge chunk from Rod Garner, who bought out half the rides. Getting those camels was one of the smartest things Abby ever did. They've allowed the ranch to stay in the black even through tough times."

Preston paced the room restlessly. "As Navajos we're taught that everything is part of a larger pattern, even good and evil. Falcon lets me see what others miss, but these events are impossible to piece together."

"That's because key elements are still coming to the surface," Kyle said.

"Someone's trying to scare Abby away from the ranch. That's a given. The rest is murky. There's a corporation interested in her land, but it would use their business connections and economic muscle—all legal. Why risk breaking the law by trying to scare her out?"

"*That's* what's really bothering you, bro," Daniel said. "This is your beat, and knowing that someone's threatening a woman right under your nose is making you crazy."

"It's more than that," Kyle said quietly, looking at Preston. "You really like this woman, don't you?"

"Okay, you've got me. I like her, probably more than I should," he admitted grudgingly. "Abby touches a lot of lives and makes a difference. I respect that. For instance, there's a kid who hangs around there, a Navajo boy named Bobby Neskahi. He's in foster care. Right now the ranch is his real lifeline."

"Speaking of Bobby, you asked me to check up on him," Daniel said. "I got some background, but it's all unofficial. I couldn't access anything that's under Child Services, and I didn't feel right hacking into those files."

"I can respect that," Preston said. "Show me what you have."

Daniel manipulated files and commands on the display surface and sent a new screen onto the wall monitor. "Bobby's mother died when he was three. He continued to live with his dad, but the man had a serious gambling problem—and one

Chapter Sixteen

Driving over in two vehicles, they took the truck bypass around Hartley and made it in twenty minutes. After verifying via phone that Abby and Bobby were okay, Preston coasted into the parking lot, engine turned off to avoid making noise. As Abby had said, no vehicles except hers were on the grounds and he could see no one in the immediate area. The volunteers wouldn't arrive until later, during feeding time, and with no kids on the premises, Michelle wasn't on the grounds either.

Preston's brothers had parked along the road. They were going to come onto the ranch via the west flank of the basically rectangular property. Preston moved in silently, using the buildings to screen his approach. They'd all agreed to give the suspect some room and see if they could figure out exactly what he was after before moving in.

Preston soon spotted a figure in the shadow of the barn. He watched as the person, a man, judging from his size and stride, slipped around the near corner and headed to Abby's hay truck, which was parked across from the barn.

"He's by the hay truck," Preston whispered into his phone to Daniel and Kyle.

Using the barn itself to screen him, Preston cut across the yard and reached the shadows where the man had stood only seconds earlier. Another fifty feet and he'd be close enough to recognize a face—if the person turned around.

When the man fished something out of his jacket pocket, Preston's muscles tightened. A small bottle with a rag hanging from it could be only one thing—a homemade fire bomb.

Preston stepped out of the shadow of the barn and called out. "Police officer! Place the bomb on the ground, then step away from it and get down on your knees."

The man, his face still hidden by the hoodie and sunglasses, set the bottle on the ground. Then, instead of doing as he'd been ordered, the guy cut around the truck and bolted north, racing down the row of outdoor enclosures.

Daniel broke radio silence. "We see him. Kyle and I will cut him off before he reaches the far end."

Preston remained in pursuit, narrowing the distance. Far ahead, he could see Daniel and Kyle climbing a corral fence at the north end. The intruder was caught in the middle.

Just then the man stopped, opened a stall gate and started yelling. The two horses inside spooked and ran out at full speed. Preston had to leap onto the fence and dive over the rails as the animals raced past him, snorting and bucking.

The suspect had reached the camels by then and threw open their gate. He started yelling again, but this time the animals held their heads up high into the air and just stared at him. The guy grabbed a lead rope draped over the fence and hit one, yelling as he did. Both camels thundered past him, racing toward Kyle and Daniel at the far end.

Going down the line, he spooked the animals in two more enclosures. Preston had to jump over the fence and into a turnout area to avoid being trampled again, and when he looked back, the intruder had disappeared.

As Kyle and Daniel worked their way up the fence line slowly, the animals began to calm down. Preston met his brother about halfway, talking softly as he passed each wild-eyed animal.

"Are you okay?" Daniel asked. "Those first two horses almost ran you down."

"Yeah, I'm just pissed off." Preston turned to look back at the ranch house and saw a uniformed officer coming up with Abby right behind him.

"I heard the animals going nuts. What happened?" She looked around and inhaled sharply. "Where are the rest of them?"

"The intruder opened the gates, then spooked them half to death. He used the confusion to get away," Preston said.

"I've got to get all of the animals back into their pens. They'll come to me, but if they're worked up and scared, they may be hard for anyone else to catch. I don't know if the gate out front is open or closed either, with all the coming and going. I need to keep them from wandering out onto the road and causing an accident or getting hurt."

"Where's Bobby now?" Preston asked.

"He's safe back at the house. The doors are locked," she said. "I've already called his foster mom and she'll be picking him up shortly."

"Give me your keys," he said. "Then call and tell Bobby that a uniformed officer is coming to meet him."

Preston looked at the officer and gave him the house keys. As the officer went to check on Bobby, Preston glanced at his brothers. "Stick around, guys."

"Sure thing. We'll search outside the grounds and herd any animals headed toward the highway back in this direction," Kyle said.

"The camels probably didn't go far," she answered. "They're a bit barn sour and don't like to leave a familiar place. Let me get some lead ropes, halters and treats to lure them in."

Once they reached the driveway, Preston studied the tracks. "The horses headed north, but the camels went west."

"We'll round up the horses," Daniel said. "We know how to handle them."

Abby gave them several halters and lead ropes, and they split up.

"I'm pretty sure I know where Hank and Eli went," she said. As they walked down the road in the opposite direction of the highway, she pointed straight ahead. "I walk them down that arroyo sometimes, and they feed on the brush. Once we spot them I'll get Hank. You take Eli."

"How will I be able to tell them apart?" Preston asked, noting the camel tracks led in the direction of the arroyo, as Abby had predicted.

"Eli's quieter. Hanks more vocal and likely to kick if he's angry or agitated. Considering a camel can kick in four directions, those feet are quite a weapon."

They left the highway and started walking up the wide ten-foot-deep wash, which was dry and sandy on the bottom at the moment. The camel tracks led down the meandering channel to a sharp right-hand curve.

Daniel called in a short time later and Preston put him on speaker. "We've gathered up three of the horses and can see two others back at the ranch, behind the barn. Guess they never got out."

"That's great," Abby said. "Which ones got out completely?"

"Well, one's Big Red and he knows me. I grabbed his mane, and I'm leading him in. The other two are following, and Kyle's back there with them. They're the oldest ones, I think."

"That'll be Missy and Tracker. They're very gentle and will just follow along," she said, loud enough for her voice to carry.

Before Daniel could answer, she heard a familiar squeak from around the curve.

"That sounds like a dog toy but out here?" Preston said.

She smiled and shook her head. "That's actually Hank's alarm call. I need to let him know it's me."

They hurried to the curve in the arroyo channel, and about a hundred feet ahead they could see the camels. Preston stopped as Abby moved closer to them.

"Hank, I've got treats," Abby called out. "Come on. Butterscotch ones! Time to go home." She stopped and waited.

Both camels came toward them, ambling down the sand-layered arroyo.

"That's a good boy," she said and held out the treats. "Let's go home, boys," she said, haltering both and giving Eli's lead rope to Preston.

"I feel like Lawrence of Arabia," he muttered.

"They're great here in the desert. Low maintenance compared to a horse and a lot gentler. Takes a lot to rile a camel, but once you do, they don't forget."

It took another hour to get all the animals back into their stalls and check to make sure none were injured.

"Since we've got the place to ourselves right now," Daniel told Abby, "I'd like to set up a couple of cameras. They won't feed into our monitors back at the office, but they'll record. The others can be put up later, but I think we need something for right now."

"That's fine," she said.

As Kyle and Daniel drove off in Kyle's pickup, Abby glanced back at the house. "Bobby's still inside the house and I bet he's scared, even with the officer there."

"Let me go," Preston said. "I'll release the patrolman and talk things over with Bobby until his foster parents pick him up. The boy did a real good job today, spotting the intruder like that."

As Preston headed back, Abby slipped into the camel pen to remove their halters. Feeling really down, she leaned against Hank, fighting the tears forming in her eyes. What was happening? Up to now, Sitting Tall Ranch had been a dream come true. She'd led an almost perfect life, giving kids time away from their challenges and becoming part of a community she'd learned to love. Now she couldn't even keep her own animals safe!

Hank made a soft gurgling noise, as if to comfort her. "I'm okay, Hank. I'm glad you are, too."

Abby went to the barn and hung the halters in the remodeled stall that served as their tack room. Hearing a sound behind her, she spun around, her heart at her throat. That's when she saw it was only Charley, the donkey, poking his head over the door of his stall.

Abby took a breath, but instead of calming down, she began to tremble, and no matter how hard she tried, she couldn't seem to stop. Leaning against the door of the tack room, she slid downward until she was in a sitting position, her arms around herself. She rocked herself silently for a moment or two, scarcely aware of what she was doing.

Abby wasn't sure how long she'd stayed there, but when she heard Preston calling her name, she wiped her face quickly and stood. "I'm over here, in the tack room."

Preston walked up, took one look at her and pulled her into his arms. "Today was a win, Abby. Sure, he got away, but we kept him from doing any harm."

"I usually don't fall to pieces like this, Preston, but I just don't know how to deal with what's happening."

"I do. Let me handle it."

"But I'm running out of time. I put everything I have into this ranch, and I can't lose it now. If I do, then Sandy…" She buried her head against his shoulder and said nothing more.

"What about Sandy?"

"One of the many things this ranch does is keep Sandy's memory alive for me," she whispered. "It was my way of affirming that her death brought about at least one good thing. If I lose it…"

"You won't lose the memory of your sister or of anyone you love. That's inside you, safe and sound," Preston said. "No matter what happens to this ranch tomorrow, next week or in thirty years, Abby, you've already won. You took your dream, made it real and shared it with a lot of kids."

"But I might not be able to hold on to Sitting Tall Ranch and that possibility terrifies me. It would be like losing a piece of my heart. I've tried to be strong, but…"

"Everyone can use a helping hand from time to time. That doesn't make you weak. It makes you human." He walked with her to the house, keeping her close to his side. "In fact, I've got a great idea. Let me move into the bunkhouse until the case is closed."

"No, the ranch is too dangerous now. I have to stay, but not you."

"I can handle danger. I'm a police officer and that's what I do," he said. "Falcon will be right there to help me, too."

"Is he one of your brothers?" she asked.

Preston smiled. "In a way," he said, going back into the house with her. "Falcon is my spiritual brother." He reached into his shirt and lifted the leather cord around his neck. A small pouch hung from it. He opened it and took out a black fetish carved out of jet. "This is Falcon, *Hosteen* Silver's gift to me. Its magic will protect you, too," he said, holding it in the palm of his hand.

"Tell me more about Falcon." She took the delicately carved bird, studied it for a moment, then returned it to him.

Abby watched him place it back carefully in the pouch as she waited. She wanted to know everything about this man who was so gentle with her, yet could become such a fierce protector the instant danger closed in.

"All but one of us—Paul—got the fetish on our sixteenth

birthday," he said, taking a seat on the sofa. "For me, my foster father chose Falcon because when my brothers fought, I'd be the one who stepped in to break it up."

"That sounds like a dangerous thing to do," she said.

"Nah, we knew each other's moves too well," he said, chuckling. "Sometimes I'd take a misplaced hit, but we never went all out with family."

"How does Falcon fit in with the role of peacemaker?"

"Falcon is about harmony and the value of hard work. Since he hunts close to the ground, Falcon focuses his searches and sees what others might miss. He shares that gift with me and that's helped make me a good detective."

"I wonder if I could get a falcon fetish for myself. If I can see trouble coming, it might help me get through this."

Preston shook his head. "Falcon's not right for you, but I think I know what would be a good match. I'll bring it to you."

"I'd love that, but I should be giving *you* a thank-you gift, not the other way around. You're even willing to stay in the bunkhouse and I know that wouldn't be easy for you. Beliefs like the *chindi* are part of your culture. You may not believe in it, but you still respect it."

"Yeah, I do," he said with a nod, "but as a cop, I've learned to work around it." He brushed the side of her face with his palm. "I'm needed here."

"I do need you," she whispered, then stood on tiptoes and brushed a gentle kiss on his lips.

It had only been meant as a tender expression of gratitude but his reaction was fierce and swift. He grabbed a fistful of her hair and pulled her to him.

A delicious fire coursed through her when he parted her lips and deepened the kiss. She didn't resist. Giving in to temptation, she melted into him as he lay back on the couch and pulled her over him.

With each heartbeat, his touch became rougher and his

kiss burned hotter. Then to her complete surprise, he eased his hold and helped her sit up.

Bewildered, it took her a moment to gather her wits. Taking a shaky breath, she looked into his eyes and saw the iron-willed control he held over himself.

"I'm sorry," she said, straightening her clothing and moving away from him. "You didn't start this, and I can see you don't want to…"

"I don't *want* to?" He laughed, a dark, edgy sound that sent its vibrations all through her. "I won't take more because you're not ready for what I have to offer." He stood. "Abby, you're a good person. You live in a world of light and hope, but my world's rough and dirty. I can't give you anything except moments, and you deserve more than that."

"I haven't asked for promises. I need your strength and you want…my softness. Why is that wrong? I know you have feelings for me. I can feel it in here," she said, pointing to her heart.

"I'm trying to protect you," he said, his face tense, his mouth set, "but I'm just a man. Don't push me."

"It doesn't seem I can," she said in an unsteady voice. "Maybe if I dressed differently—more feminine, showing myself off more…"

"Abby, I'm trying to give you a break. I want you. I care about you more than I should. You need to be protected—even from me."

"You want me…" She said it slowly, savoring the words.

"How could you doubt it?"

"Then just let go. *Show* me what you feel."

Her words broke his control and he hauled her into his arms. He kissed her roughly, crushing her lips and drinking her in.

She gasped as he left her mouth and rained kisses down the

column of her throat. His hand tangled into her hair, urging her head back and exposing her to more of his kisses.

With rough hands he worked her blouse open easily, then with the expertise of a man who'd been with many women, undid her bra in one fluid motion.

When he pressed his mouth to the tip of her breast, her knees almost buckled, but he held her against him, letting his touch burn into her.

She loved the feel of his calloused hands on her. To be wanted by this man who was all passion and courage…nothing could be better than that. Somehow she found herself braced against the wall as he removed the rest of her clothing, kissing all the areas he exposed.

Preston found her hidden places, and she whimpered helplessly as sensations too powerful to resist washed over her. That burning…that need…

"I can't stand up anymore," she said in a ragged voice. "I'm going to fall."

"Hold on to my shoulders," he said, tasting her until she came apart.

In one wonderful moment of pure pleasure, her world shattered. Too weak to stand, she would have fallen if he hadn't risen to his feet and held her tightly against him.

After several moments, her breathing evened.

"That's what's in my heart," he murmured.

When she looked into his eyes, she saw the fire that still raged inside him. "Stop holding back. Let go," she whispered. "I need to feel you inside me, taking and giving me everything."

He had no words. He was past thinking. He kissed her hard, his heart thundering.

Feeling her tug at his clothing with trembling hands, he helped her, shrugging out of his shirt and then unbuckling his belt. Every time her fingertips brushed his skin he grew harder and moved closer to the edge.

He could have taken her right there, but this was Abby. He wanted more. For her. For him. "Easy…" he murmured. "Bed?"

"Down the hall, to the left."

"To the pink bedroom?"

"Yes."

He lifted her into his arms and carried Abby to her room.

He set her down gently on the bed, but before he could lie next to her, she held her hand out. "Wait. Can I just look at you?"

"If that's what you want," he said, sucking in a breath as her gaze seared over him.

"Your tattoo?"

His laugh was a husky growl. He turned around to reveal that over the base of his spine was the word *Naalzheehí*.

"It means hunter," he said. "My brother Rick and I went out one night with Conner, a Special Forces buddy of ours. We came up with secret tribal war names for each other, like the *Diné* warriors of old. Conner's uncle took care of the tattoos as part of a ritual."

"The hunter…but why place it there?" she asked with a bemused smile.

"A war name is a source of power that must remain secret from all except those you trust. The spine symbolizes a man's strength. It seemed fitting."

She held out her arms to him, inviting him onto the bed. "Tonight, you're not a hunter…you're just…mine."

He lay over her, but she pushed him back gently, kissing him with infinite tenderness. Her caresses nearly broke him. No woman had ever treated him with this sweet care.

Abby didn't just leave a trail of moist kisses down his body—she loved him with each caress. Her touch was exquisite torture, and as she explored his body, trying to please him, fire coursed through his veins.

"No more," he said, sucking in a breath. Taking her in his arms, he rolled over, positioning her beneath him.

As he slipped inside her softness, he heard her gasp. Somehow he forced himself to slow down, but when her fingers dug into his buttocks and she arched up, he was lost.

He clamped his hands over hers and held her as he took her and finished what was meant to be.

His breathing evened slowly. He wasn't sure how long he'd lain on top of her when he finally shifted and gathered her against him. Seeing the dreamy and contented look on her face, he smiled.

"You were right," she said.

"About what?"

"Pink, you don't like the color, but it didn't matter."

He laughed. "I had more important things on my mind."

"Will you stay, even if I fall asleep?"

"Yes. Just close your eyes and listen to my heartbeat." He brushed a kiss over her forehead and held her.

He woke up hours later and watched her sleep. As a disposable kid and a cop, he'd seen too much of life to believe anything called love could ever last. Sure, Abby needed him now, but after harmony was restored, there'd be no room in her life for a cop. All he could bring to the mix was darkness.

Some things were just not meant to be. He tightened his hold on her. Happiness was elusive, and that meant you needed to live moment by moment.

This was as good as it got. For tonight, she was his.

Chapter Seventeen

Abby woke up in Preston's arms. They'd made love, rested, then made love again. Now it was close to dawn and her life, with all its demands, would soon call to her.

She stirred slightly and gazed at him. Though she'd fallen in love with Preston, she knew his feelings for her were more...complicated. He'd made love to her with his body but had kept at least a part of his heart out of her reach. That was something that might never change.

Yet no matter what, he'd still cared enough for her to risk his job, something she knew meant everything to him. The knowledge filled her with a fierce sense of protectiveness and love.

He opened his eyes. "Checking me out—again?"

She laughed. "I'm worried about you."

He laughed. "You destroyed me last night, but I think I can still function."

"That's not what I meant," she said, poking him in the ribs. "Be serious."

"I was," he said, laughing.

"Your superiors will be angry."

"I wasn't planning to tell them," Preston said.

"What if they find out?"

"I'll say you needed protection, and I volunteered."

"I can talk to the mayor if you get into trouble. He's one

of our biggest donors and he loves the ranch." She sat up and met his gaze. "If you have a problem, I'll help you. I promise."

"Stop worrying." He checked his watch and gave her a quick kiss. "I need to stop by my place and get a clean change of clothes, then I'll have to go by the station. I'll get Kyle to come over while I'm gone. One of us will be here from now on."

"If your brother says no—"

He kissed her again. "My brother won't say no to me. We're there for each other. End of story."

He got up, pulled on his jeans, then fished out his cell phone from his shirt pocket and dialed Kyle. "I need you at the ranch," he said. "I want round-the-clock protection for Abby." He listened to Kyle's response, then hung up. "All set. He'll be here in thirty."

"I'll make some coffee," she said, then realizing she was naked, tugged at the sheet.

He laughed. "You're shy now?"

"It's daylight."

"And?" he pressed.

"My body's not perfect."

"It is to me," he said, pulling the sheet away from her. "Just perfect."

She laughed, still self-conscious as his gaze took her in slowly and thoroughly. "Detective, we both work for a living, so we better get going. Behave." She reached for her robe, then hurried to the kitchen. "Eggs? Toast?"

"No, just juice and coffee."

He came into the kitchen moments later, phone to his ear. "Coffee?" he mouthed.

She handed him a cup, and he continued speaking to whomever was on the other line.

"I'll be in to question him shortly."

Preston placed the phone back in his shirt pocket, came

closer and parted her robe so he could gaze at her. "As I said, beautiful."

She felt her knees go weak.

"I have to go," he said, giving her a slow, deep kiss. "Think of me."

With that, he was gone. Abby leaned back against the counter and took a breath. It was like standing in the middle of a tornado. Everything around her was falling apart, but in the center, for a moment, there was love.

ABBY WAS OUT feeding the animals less than fifteen minutes later. It was seven in the morning and already she was running behind. Usually by this time she would have had at least two volunteers present but, today, no one was around.

After mucking out the llama and donkey stalls and feeding the animals, she heard a truck pulling up near the barn. She glanced over and saw Michelle.

"Where do you want me to start?" Michelle asked, hurrying over to meet her.

"I've gotten the llamas and donkeys taken care of, except for topping off their water troughs. The camels and horses are still waiting their turn."

Michelle looked around. "Where are the volunteers? It's summer. Monroe and a handful of kids should have been here by now."

"I know, but I suspect word got out that we had problems again yesterday," she said, updating her.

"I haven't seen or read the news, but reporters monitor police channels so I'm willing to bet that's how the story got out." Michelle took a deep breath. "I've been meaning to ask you something, Abby. Are you planning to sell the ranch? I saw Stan looking around the place a few days ago, and he told me he was working up an offer for you."

"Stan did make me a fair offer, but I'm not selling, Michelle. I'm making my stand here. The ranch and I obviously have enemies, but we still have a lot of friends."

As she glanced back at the house she saw Kyle. He appeared to be casually looking at the animals, but she knew he was here ready to help in case of trouble. Taking comfort from the thought, she got back to work.

PRESTON SAT AT the breakfast counter and sipped a strong cup of coffee. He'd stopped by his house to get some more clothes, passed by the station and was now at his brother Daniel's place.

"Paul says he's going to cut his honeymoon short and help us out," Daniel said.

Preston shook his head. "He shouldn't do that. He's been through enough and deserves time off. Tell him to stay put next time you hear from him."

"I will, but he may not listen. Gene's sticking around, too. He's still in the shower, I think. We're with you, bro. I also spoke to Rick last night via a video connection. He really wanted to come, too, but he can't swing it. He did say that he plans to be home in a few months, and this time he's going to stay," Daniel said.

"We all know he's in the FBI, currently overseas, but do you realize that you're the only one who has any idea what he does?"

"Yeah, but it's not like he confided in me. I found out by accident."

"How the heck did you do that?" Preston asked.

Daniel shook his head. "Can't say. I got a few calls afterward though. Glad I had DOD clearance."

Gene walked into the room shirtless, barefooted and holding a mug of steaming coffee. "This coffee will wake up the dead. By the time I finish, I'll be ready to work. Where do you need me today?"

Preston smiled. That was the thing about being one of *Hosteen* Silver's foster sons. You never had to ask for backup. It was there the moment trouble appeared, sometimes before.

"I'd like to toss some ideas around first. I still don't have a handle on this case. Someone wants Abby to shut down the ranch, but there's nothing there that's particularly valuable and worth all the trouble. All I've got is an admitted purchase offer from her accountant who wants to resell the property to a corporation that may or may not be coming to the area," he said. "Basically, I've got zip."

"All this time you've been searching for evidence linked to the murder, but let's try a different angle," Daniel said. "Let's look at the ranch through the eyes of the intruder. He wasn't after Abby, so where was he heading? We need to walk around those areas and see what's there."

"Good idea," Gene said.

"Let's go to the ranch and take a closer look." Preston stood and checked that he had his phone and weapon in place. "Time to go." Confidence high, he walked to the door. When *Hosteen's* boys came together, nothing stood in their way for long. Abby didn't realize it yet, but the best of the best were on her side.

PRESTON ARRIVED AT the ranch minutes ahead of Daniel and Gene. As he stepped out of the SUV he saw Kyle standing in the shade by the barn and tying knots with a lead rope. It was all very casual, but Preston knew it was his brother's way of standing guard without seeming to do so.

Seeing Abby in one of the empty stalls, Preston went to join her. "You've only got three helpers today?" he asked, glancing at Bobby, Monroe and Michelle, who were grooming horses.

She nodded, brushing hay off her sleeves, then fastening her hair into a ponytail. "Monroe just showed up, but he'll have to leave soon. The bad publicity is killing me, Preston.

Rod said he's going to free Ilse's time so she can come help more often, but I'm barely holding my own right now."

"Things will turn around soon," he said, resisting the urge to take her hand and reassure her with his touch.

Seeing Daniel and Gene walking up the sidewalk, Abby greeted them with a smile. "What's going on, guys?"

"We're going to join forces and figure out why someone's targeting the ranch. One possibility is that there's something here someone considers a threat or wants so much they're willing to kill to get it. We're going to look around and see what we can find," Preston said.

Bobby came around the corner of a stack of hay bales and walked over to join Preston. "I'm back now, so I can help you. I'll notice if anything's been added or taken away recently."

"Good idea. It'll give us an extra set of eyes familiar with the place. Come on then," Preston said, leading the way inside the barn storage areas.

"What's behind that closed door?" Gene asked, pointing.

"Leather bridles, tack, saddles, things like that," Abby said.

Preston tried the door handle. "It's not locked," he said, looking at Abby.

"It's not meant to be. We keep the leather in that room to keep it clean. A lot of hay and dust flies around when we're mucking out the stalls, and I like things in top condition and clean when we saddle up for the kids."

Preston opened the door and Bobby, standing beside him, sucked in his breath.

"My bridles!" Abby said. "He's cut them to pieces, and look at the cinches. They're ruined! We need this tack so the kids can ride. It took years to accumulate all this. Why does this person hate me so much?"

"I don't think it's personal, Abby," Preston said. "This is about making you miserable so you'll leave."

"But why?"

"Once we have the motive, we'll probably be able to ID the suspect," Preston said.

"We didn't put any of the cameras inside the barn, but there's one outside," Daniel said. "Let's see who came in and out of this building." He went outside and, after a moment, brought back a flash drive and attached it to his tablet PC. Unfortunately, once the nighttime images appeared, the subjects on the screen were much harder to see.

"I want to link to my computer, so I can enhance the images, but the Wi-Fi here is too weak," Daniel said.

"Let's go back to the office to view this," she suggested.

As they walked back, Preston remained beside her, and although it was killing him, he didn't touch her. He had to keep his mind on the job.

"The infrared images aren't sharp, but these cameras were quick and easy to hook up, and we needed something right away," Daniel said. "The cameras I plan to install next will have higher resolution."

Once inside her office, Daniel immediately accessed the video, and they all gathered around to watch, even Bobby.

"Those are all my people going in and out of the barn. Even when we can't see faces, I recognize them from their general build or the way they walk."

They continued watching the feed. They saw the animals being fed, then as nighttime descended, no more people were about. Eventually, they spotted a lone figure, in shades of white, gray and green, moving toward the barn. He looked behind him once, then slipped inside.

"The tack room door won't show from this camera angle so we won't be able to tell if he went inside that area or not," Daniel said.

"Play it back," Preston said and looked at Abby. "Can you tell who that is?"

"No. I can barely see him and that loose hoodie hides his build."

"I know who it is," Bobby said.

They all looked at him.

"I can't see his face," he added quickly, "but look how he moves his shoulder in a circle, like he's trying to work out some kinks. That's Monroe. I'm sure of it. He hurt his rotator cuff chopping firewood on a camping trip and it still bugs him. I've seen him do that lots of times."

"Wait a sec, guys," Abby said. "Monroe's the police chief's son. He's one of my hardest-working volunteers and he's always the last to leave. Just because he went into the barn after hours doesn't mean he vandalized the tack. He'd have no reason to do something like that."

"Monroe was here when we arrived. You think he's still here?" Preston asked.

"Probably. If I'm around, he usually lets me know before he takes off," Abby said.

"I need to talk to him," Preston said, remembering that Ilse and Monroe had been meeting on the sly.

"There's no way Monroe's responsible for what happened," Abby said. "Let me go with you and we'll both talk to him."

"No, this is police business." He could see the worry and fear in her eyes. Abby needed to believe that people were basically good and that right always prevailed. He'd been that way once, too—naive, trying to see the best in everyone. That had died the day his mother abandoned him.

Reality was a hard teacher. As a cop, he dealt with the worst in human nature almost every day and sometimes the good guys lost. That darkness had taken its toll on him, and bringing it into Abby's life could destroy the woman he loved. He had to solve this case quickly, then move on.

Chapter Eighteen

As Preston approached, Monroe was emptying the wheelbarrow into the compost pile. "A word," Preston said.

Monroe set the handles down and turned to face him. "Something wrong?"

"Why don't you tell me?" Preston said, his voice deadly.

Monroe took a step back, refusing to look him in the eye. His face was turning red, but Preston couldn't tell if it was anger, fear or embarrassment at the thought of getting caught. It didn't matter.

"There's no place for you to go, kid. Don't even think of running," Preston growled, shifting to the side and trapping Monroe between him and the pipe fencing.

"You know, don't you?" Monroe whispered. "One word of this gets out and my dad will go nuclear. That's why I couldn't tell you."

"Go on," Preston said, wondering where this was all going.

"Ilse is ten years older than me, but that woman's *hot*. The night Carl was killed we were both here late. She and I…well, it's not really serious, but we'd been messing around. We'd meet here sometimes after everyone else was gone and Abby had turned in. That night in particular I really needed to talk to Ilse. I got engaged to someone else after some heavy-duty pressure from my parents, and I wanted to give Ilse the news myself—basically end it."

"She never mentioned being here," Preston said.

"We agreed never to tell anyone about that night or our meetings here. She was just keeping her word. Besides, neither one of us saw or heard anything that could help you find Carl's killer."

"Who else was around that night?"

Monroe shook his head. "We didn't see anyone. We went into the hay barn, then spread a tarp on the ground and...said goodbye. After an hour or so we both went home."

"You saw her leave?"

"She was getting into her car as I left."

Preston nodded slowly, his gaze still on the kid. "So why did you sneak back in here last night?"

Preston saw the kid turn a shade paler.

"How..."

"Don't waste my time," Preston snapped.

"I got a text from Ilse asking me to meet her. I was afraid she'd get angry and tell someone else about us if I didn't come, so I hurried over. She never showed up. That's when I checked the text message again and realized it was an old one I'd forgotten to delete." He brought out his cell. "I guess I was hoping I'd be a little harder to forget."

Preston almost burst out laughing. The kid had moved on, but he still wanted Ilse pining for him. "Guy, she's out of your league. Chalk it up as a pleasant experience and let it go."

"Yeah, I know," he said, "but it's harder than it sounds."

Daniel joined Preston as Monroe walked away. "I heard."

Preston chuckled softly. "That poor kid. He still has a thing for Ilse, but the chief and his wife are making him go in another direction. Smart people."

"So what now?"

"Install those other cameras here as soon as possible. In the meantime, I need to talk to Abby."

"Be careful," Daniel said in a quiet voice.

Preston stopped in midstride. "What do you mean?"

"You're hard as nails—the one brother who never lowers his guard—but you're different around this woman."

He thought of denying it but then changed his mind. "Yeah, maybe so, but it's not a forever thing. I just want to make sure she wins this fight."

"We'll be right there with you every step of the way."

"Glad you said that, bro, because there's something I need you to do for me."

PRESTON STOPPED BY the station for the second time that day to check in with the lab people. After getting some updates, he realized that what the case needed now was legwork.

As he walked back to his SUV, he checked his watch. He wanted to run one personal errand before getting back to work. Abby's courage had been continually tested and she'd held her own, but there was one more thing he could do to help her fight.

Preston drove into town and parked at the curb in front of a small store on Second Street called Southwest Treasures. Pablo Ortiz, a short, rotund man with gray hair and an easy smile, greeted him from behind the old-style oak-and-glass counter. The Zuni man had carved the fetishes he and his brothers all wore.

"What brings you here today?" he asked as Preston searched beneath the glass, studying the array of small fetishes there.

"I'm looking for White Wolf," he said.

"That's a special fetish. It'll only fit someone who's willing to protect her territory and her family at any cost," Ortiz said.

"*Hosteen* Silver told us about it. It was the one worn by the only woman he ever loved," Preston said.

"This morning I finished polishing one I carved from white turquoise, a stone as rare as White Wolf herself."

Pablo brought it out and showed Preston the intricate carving. It had delicate features and showed a standing wolf, ready for the hunt. Courage and passion were evident in its pose.

"This is perfect. I'll take it."

Ortiz placed the small fetish in a medicine pouch but not before sprinkling it with corn pollen. "This will feed its spirit and keep it strong."

"Thank you, uncle," he said, using the title out of respect.

It was almost dinnertime and he was on his way back to his SUV when his phone rang. It was Abby. He picked it up quickly.

"Everything okay?" he asked.

"Yes. Daniel set up another camera by the house that'll feed into his computer. He'd planned to hook it up somewhere else, then decided I needed it here more," she said.

"I'm glad he was able to do that."

"I also wanted you to know that I've asked Kyle to give Bobby a ride home."

"So you're alone?" he asked quickly.

"Not completely, no. Michelle is around. She took one of the horses out on a training ride, but she'll be back in a while," she said. "I just needed a little time to myself, Preston," she said calmly. "I'll be here at the house and can call 911 if necessary. One of the new cameras your brother put up also monitors the area around the house. I'll be fine."

"I get where you're coming from," he said after a beat, "but I wish you hadn't done that."

After hanging up, he looked at the medicine pouch. He'd respect her need to be alone and catch up with her later. His brother's camera would let them know almost instantly if anything went wrong.

ABBY LOOKED AROUND the living room, enjoying the stillness of the moment. Realizing that she'd become afraid to be by herself, she'd intuitively known that she had to face that fear as quickly as possible. With precautions in place, she was glad for a little time to think things through.

She'd just sat down on the couch when she heard a knock at her door. She sighed. This had to have been the shortest alone time in history.

"It's me—Michelle. Do you have a second?"

Abby opened the door and invited her inside. "Hi, Michelle. How did the ride go? Any problems?"

"No, not at all. Big Red's a great mount. That horse has a kind spirit and does his best to protect his rider."

"So what's bothering you?" she asked, noting that Michelle seemed ill at ease.

"I'm going to have to cut the hours I'm spending at the ranch and get a part-time job elsewhere. I was hoping to hold my riding classes here and pick up some extra money, but I don't have enough kids signing up."

"Because you're teaching here?"

"Maybe. I don't know. I've stopped trying to figure things out, I just deal with what's in front of me," she said.

"That's actually really good advice," Abby said, "but if what you want is a steadier paycheck, I may be able to help. With Carl gone, I'm going to need a new head wrangler, and the animals here love you. Will you take his place? The pay isn't great, but you'll have lodging."

Her expression lit up instantly. "That would be terrific."

"It may be a week or two before you can start, though. We'll need to clear out the bunkhouse and Carl's office and that'll mean going through everything there. The police may want to monitor that process, so I'll have to ask."

"I can wait, and if you need help with all that, just let me know."

Michelle started heading to the door, then stopped and turned around. "You've helped me out several times, Abby, and I'd like to do something for you in return. I know you trust Detective Bowman, and you may even be falling for him, but I've heard some things about him that you need to know."

"Like what?"

"The man's in love with his job. That always comes first."

She smiled. "And I'm in love with this ranch."

"It's more complicated than that. Your life here at the ranch, under ordinary circumstances, is a peaceful one, and that's one of the many things you love about it. Detective Bowman's a cop. He probably chose that job because of the promise of danger and excitement," she said. "Abby, face it—you two are as compatible as snow and summer sunshine."

"That's why he won't be around after the case is closed," she said softly. "I've known that from the start."

"It's already too late for warnings, isn't it?"

"I'll be fine," she said, walking Michelle outside and back to her pickup. "See you tomorrow."

As Michelle drove off, Abby glanced up at one of the new cameras. It was well hidden, mounted high underneath a roof overhang, melding into the afternoon shadows but pointed at the house and its immediate surroundings.

She was walking back, lost in thought, when she saw one of the horses pacing, head down. Afraid that the horse might have the beginnings of colic, she hurried over to his pen. A closer look told her that the animal wasn't sick. Abby glanced around, trying to figure out what was bothering him, and caught a glimpse of a shadowy figure going around the barn.

Afraid for her animals, Abby looked up at the camera, pointed ahead, then quietly headed toward the figure, cell phone in hand. Daniel, or whoever was monitoring the feed, would now know she was on the move, and on the way she'd call 911.

Unless her animals were threatened, she intended to stay behind cover, but she wanted to get a look at the person who was causing so many problems for her. Hopefully, it would turn out to be a stranger, not a traitor associated with her ranch.

Abby followed him as he headed past the pens and toward the shed just beyond the barn. Realizing he wasn't after her animals, she decided to stay well back and stopped near the bales of straw they'd eventually use for bedding. When he passed by on his way back out, she'd be able to see his face and still remain hidden.

Minutes ticked by. Soon she heard a car pulling up, tires crunching on the gravel. She turned around to see who it was, but her shoulder struck a bale and the thump gave away her position.

Before she could move away, the intruder jumped her from behind and tackled her to the ground.

Abby fought back, kicking and trying to turn her head around to get a look at his face. As he pushed her back to the ground, he scraped her forehead.

Stunned, she turned her face away. It had to have been a watch or a ring. She'd felt the pain of hard metal.

Hearing approaching footsteps, Abby cried out. "Help! Over here!"

Her attacker jumped up and disappeared around the corner.

Abby sat up slowly, touching the dampness of blood on her forehead.

Preston ran up just then. "You're hurt," he said, seeing the trickle of blood running down her face.

"I'm fine. Go! Hurry! The guy ducked around the side of the barn."

"I'LL BE BACK." As Preston ran over, he saw the back door of the hay storage area swinging shut, but no one was around. He raced down the front of the stalls, passing the animals at a sprint. Suddenly he struck something with his foot, tripped and hurtled facedown onto the ground with a thud.

He scrambled back up, anticipating an ambush, then spotted the rake the suspect had obviously tossed into the path. He'd been checking the stalls as he passed and had missed the handle in the darkness.

Spinning around, he looked for the suspect. None of the animals appeared unduly alarmed, and there was no movement on the other side of the grounds. The runner was gone, and he had no idea which direction to search. Maybe the man had doubled back.

Preston raced back to the other end of the barn. He had to make sure Abby was still safe. He turned the far corner and saw her still sitting there, holding a tissue to the cut on her forehead.

Before she could protest he lifted her into his arms. "I'm carrying you back to the house."

Chapter Nineteen

Under the bright lights of her kitchen, Preston cleaned and inspected the long but shallow cut just above Abby's brow. "It's a head wound so it's going to bleed a while, but it's not deep," he said, dabbing it with a damp paper towel.

Abby saw that his hands were shaking. Preston had a gentle heart, though he seldom let anyone see that side of him.

"I'm fine," she said. "If I hadn't been distracted, I might have been able to give you a better description of his face. All I can tell you for sure is that he was wearing some kind of weird makeup—green and black—in splotches."

"They sell that stuff for bow hunters nowadays to break up their facial patterns, but this guy isn't hunting deer. He's afraid of being recognized," Preston said.

Seeing that the cut had stopped bleeding, he finally took a deep breath. "I have to go back there and take a look around. I want to know what he was after."

"He was headed to the shed by the barn, but I keep it locked. It's not that there's anything of great value in there. I just don't want the kids inside. I have ant poison and things like that in there."

"This confirms my theory," Preston said. "The suspect's after something he believes is here at the ranch. He wants to run you out because he needs the freedom to roam at will and look for whatever it is. It also explains why he stayed around so long after killing Carl that night."

"He was still searching. I wish I knew what he's after. I'd cheerfully hand it over to him if he'd leave me and the ranch alone."

Preston grabbed a powerful fluorescent lantern she kept on the table. "I'm going to borrow this and look through the interior of the shed and barn."

"I'm going with you. Two pairs of eyes are better than one."

"Not necessary. I have Falcon's gift, remember?"

"Okay, let me rephrase—six pairs of eyes are better than four," she said.

He smiled. "Okay, let's go."

It was soon clear that the intruder had never made it inside the shed. Preston spotted a few deep marks on the door that told him he'd tried to break in. He looked for prints, but the ones he found on the knob were too smudged.

"What I still don't understand is how Carl's connected to this. Carl really cared about this ranch and its mission. He worked harder than anyone else except me."

"My gut tells me we need to focus on who he was before he came here. No one can outrun their past, Abby," he said. "Sometimes we fool ourselves into thinking we can, but it's always there, waiting for us around every corner."

"New beginnings are possible."

"Spoken like a person who has never tried to outrun something," he said.

"You're wrong. My past is filled with painful memories I wish I could leave behind, Preston. I haven't led a perfect life. You've put me on a pedestal, but I don't belong there. I've made plenty of mistakes, some that I've come to regret, and I've taken chances when I shouldn't have," she said. "But here's the thing—life goes by fast and if you spend too much time weighing all those what-ifs, you'll miss out on what's there in front of you," she said, reaching for his hand.

"Taking what's there can carry a high price…later," Preston said in a quiet voice.

"I know."

He took her into his arms and kissed her gently. "A cop's life—"

"Is perfect for you," she said, interrupting him. "You don't have to say anything else."

PRESTON SLEPT LIGHTLY and remained in the front room of her house that night. Close to dawn he got up and went outside to take a look around. He moved silently, melding into the twilight shadows. Everything appeared peaceful, but he knew in his gut that was only temporary. A storm waited in the wings.

As he headed back to the house, he heard a vehicle, then saw Kyle pulling in. His brother came over and handed him one of two cardboard cups with lids.

"I was going to down both coffees, but you look like you need some just as much as I do," Kyle said.

"You've got that right. I was up most of the night going over Carl's case file. I've given up on the idea that Carl's murder was an unpremeditated attack by a local enemy of his," Preston said. "The more I dig into the vic's past, the more gaps I find in his history."

"Like what?"

"Carl claimed he worked solo, but there's no way he could have pulled off some of those heists by himself. The one in Denver especially caught my eye. No alarm was triggered, something only possible if two wires, in two separate locations, were cut at almost the same time. I called the investigating officer. He said that Carl had no known associates, and although he was certain Carl had worked with an accomplice, they were never able to get him to change his story."

"Maybe he partnered up with his fence or had an insider who helped him out," Kyle said.

"Taking it from there, what if that person knew Carl had held on to some of the merchandise instead of splitting the take? That would explain all the searches," Preston said.

"Yeah, and Carl's partner would have been ticked off about losing his share."

"Anger would also explain getting beat up as opposed to shot. The killer came wanting answers. Of course now that Carl's dead, his logical next step is finding what Carl did with the stuff."

"Makes sense," Kyle said.

"The problem is that it's all conjecture. I've got nothing except the murder of a thief and some unexplained searches."

"There's a lot of ground to cover on this ranch." Kyle took a breath and looked around. "It could be anywhere, even buried along the fence someplace."

Preston shook his head. "No. Concentrate on the man. Everything we know about Carl tells us he was careful and paid attention to the smallest details. He would have wanted to keep stolen paintings safe and someplace he could monitor them."

"Yeah, you're right, but where do we begin?"

"Let's go take a second look at the bunkhouse and Carl's office in the barn. Focus only on places where he might have hidden a valuable painting."

Preston and Kyle had begun looking in Carl's office when Abby came in.

"I'm glad you're taking one last look around," she said. "I've promised Michelle the job of head wrangler, and that means I'll have to clear out all of Carl's things." She looked at the charcoal sketch to her right. "I'm going to keep his southwest landscapes, though."

Preston studied the drawing closest to her. "I recognize that place, but it's not laid out right." He took a closer look. "That rock formation is on the road to Shiprock, on the right-hand side, and past Kirtland, but the sketch is reversed. We're actually viewing it from behind."

"Yeah, you're right," Kyle said. "Interesting perspective."

"Something else, too," Preston said. "I remember seeing a charcoal sketch similar to this one in Stan Cooper's office."

"I know the one you're talking about, but that's not one of Carl's," Abby said. "Stan's painting is by Burt Yancy, a well-known southwest artist. Maybe that's why Carl painted it this way, so it would have his own mark."

Preston nodded but didn't say anything at first. At long last he lifted it off the hook. "It's kinda heavy considering there's no glass and the frame's just cheap plastic," he said. "I'm going to take the sketch out of this and see if there's something special about the paper."

Preston undid the back and removed the plain cardboard backing. "It's ordinary drawing paper."

"He liked to sketch, but he wasn't rich," Abby said. "You buy that stuff by the tablet, I think."

Preston remained silent. He was sure there was something he wasn't seeing—yet.

He closed his eyes for a moment, like *Hosteen* Silver had taught him to do, and concentrated, calling on Falcon to help him.

A moment later he opened his eyes. Setting the sketch aside, he examined the backing for several seconds. "Carl slit this cardboard in half, then glued it back together around the outside. There's something sandwiched inside there."

Preston worked the two layers apart carefully and pulled out another painting, an oil depicting a rodeo scene. "This one's by Whit McCabe. I don't know much about art, but I've heard that name."

"He dates back to the early 1900s," Abby said. "We studied

him in school. 'Rodeo' isn't his most popular painting, but if it's authentic, I bet that painting would bring in six figures."

"Okay, so why wasn't this ever reported as stolen?" Preston asked, lost in thought. "Then again, maybe it was, and after the insurance was collected, the case faded into the background. Art's not my specialty."

"Daniel could do a fast background check on it," Kyle said, texting Daniel and sending him a photo of the painting. "There's got to be a sales record for anything that valuable."

"I have a feeling that this is what the intruder has been looking for all along and why he's been tearing this place apart," Preston said. "Carl hid it well. It was easy to overlook. We did, even after taking it out of the frame."

"Once the news about this painting spreads, the killer won't have reason to come back here and I won't have to worry anymore."

"Not necessarily. What if—" Kyle started to say more but then clamped his mouth shut when he saw Preston shake his head, then gesture for them to meet him outside.

"Ask Daniel to come over, Kyle," he said once they were out on the sidewalk. "I want to have this place swept for bugs. The killer, probably someone who spends time here, knew Carl had something he wanted. It's possible he kept his eyes—and ears—on Carl before making his move. I would have if I were in his shoes." He looked at Abby. "I'd like to have Carl's office, bunkhouse and even your place checked for electronic listening devices. Are you okay with that, Abby?"

She nodded. "If you find something, will you be able to track it back to the killer?"

"I hope so," Preston answered.

"Do you think there are other paintings still hidden here?" She glanced at Kyle, remembering what he'd started to say, then looked back at Preston.

"It's a possibility," Preston answered.

She swallowed hard and gestured to the pickup and small sedan just pulling into the parking lot. "That's Stan in the truck and Bobby in the sedan," she said. "I should go."

"Take care of whatever you need. I'll handle things here and let you know if anything new comes up."

ABBY WALKED AWAY from Preston quickly. She'd barely held it together, and she didn't want him to see her fall apart. If everything they'd said about Carl was right, then she was at least partially responsible for the trouble the ranch was in. After all, she'd hired him.

Abby took a deep steadying breath and forced a smile as she greeted Bobby and Stan.

"Stan, what brings you here so early?" He was wearing his suit and bolo tie, so she knew he hadn't come to volunteer tending the animals. "More bad news?"

"Yeah, Abby, I'm afraid so. I went over the accounts and we need to talk."

"All right," she said, wondering how many hits a person could take and still remain standing. As she glanced over at Bobby and saw his shaky smile, she knew the answer. She would never give up.

"Let's see what the bad news is and how we can turn it around," she said, leading the way to her office.

Bobby took her hand and smiled.

"Have you had breakfast, Bobby?" she asked, knowing he tended to skip it altogether if his foster father was in a rush to get going. That's why she kept cereal and milk in the office fridge.

He shook his head. "But it's okay. I'm not hungry."

"Go to the kitchen and pour yourself a bowl of cereal anyway while Stan and I talk."

As Bobby left, Abby offered Stan a seat on the chair across from her desk.

"I made all the payments this month and checked to make sure everything went through. After I finished, I took a closer look at your cash reserves. You're in trouble, Abby. Your operating funds are lower than they've been since opening day at Sitting Tall Ranch. Painting the buildings and buying hay for the rest of the year took a chunk out of your account."

"Donations slow down in the summer and pick up in the fall. That's the way it always is."

Stan shook his head. "It's more than that, and you know it. Word's out that J&R Sports Paradise is going to buy the empty acreage next to yours. The Double T ranch is already planning to add their land to that deal rather than get a lower offer later on. If those acquisitions go through and you won't take J&R's offer, things are going to get real tough."

"I know," she said.

"J&R will go to court to have this entire area rezoned, shutting you down. They have the resources and political clout to make that happen. Your best option is to preempt that by selling out now to my investment group. That's the only way you'll have enough money to relocate. Try to fight this in court, and even if you win, the legal costs will bleed this ranch dry. You could lose everything."

"That'll never happen," she said. "This ranch has friends, too. I intend to fight."

"At least raise enough money to lawyer up. Sell some of the animals, maybe the llamas and the camels. That could buy you some good legal representation when J&R starts to get ugly."

"Those animals were donations to this ranch. I can't do that."

"Yes, you can. It's business, and it'll help you raise some cash *and* cut down on your overhead. The camels, in particular, could bring in a decent sum. There are recreation parks and zoos that would appreciate camels with training."

She swallowed hard, but not trusting her voice, she remained silent.

"You need to save what you've got, Abby. Think about it, okay?"

She walked him to the door without saying a word. Everything had gone so wrong, so fast.

After Stan left, she closed the door behind him and slumped back against it. "Don't the good guys ever win anymore?" she whispered to the empty room.

"Sure they do," Bobby said, coming in.

She straightened up immediately. "Bobby, I thought you were having breakfast."

"I was, but you and Mr. Cooper weren't whispering, so I heard what he told you," he said. "I figured you needed a friend right now."

"Bobby, listen to me. You can't tell anyone what you heard, okay? I'm not sure what I'm going to do, but I'll make things work. When I first began talking to people and asking for funds, a lot of them refused to believe Sitting Tall Ranch could ever be more than a dream." With a smile and a shrug, she added, "Sometimes you just have to follow your heart."

"I won't say anything, Abby, but you really need a rich friend, someone who can help you keep this place alive."

She smiled at him and shook her head. "The ranch can always use donors, but I'll never pick friends based on how much money they have. That's not a good way to measure someone's real worth."

Bobby thought it over, then nodded.

"Why don't you go help Michelle with the animals?" she said, then added, "Lock the door on your way out."

"Okay, Abby," he said, and left.

PRESTON MET DANIEL over by the ranch's bunkhouse, but an ingrained caution kept him glancing back in the opposite direction. He saw Stan leave Abby's office first, then Bobby came out minutes later.

"Did you hear what I just said?" Daniel asked.

"Yeah, you want to know why I didn't call the department and ask them to sweep the place," Preston said, focusing on his brother. "The reason I didn't is because I'm trying to avoid leaks to the press. That would just complicate things right now."

"I hear you. My equipment's a generation ahead of the P.D.'s anyway," he said with a quick grin.

"Our budget these days is nearly nonexistent," Preston said. "Here comes Bobby. Watch what you say around him. He's a sharp kid."

Bobby approached Preston a moment later. "Can we talk?"

"Sure," Preston said, leading him away from Daniel.

"It's about Abby. She's in trouble."

"What's going on?" Preston asked quickly.

Bobby started to say something, then shook his head. "I can't say, I promised, but I overheard some stuff. Maybe she'll tell you."

"Okay, I'll go talk to her," Preston said.

"Good. I have to help Michelle right now. Looks like I'm the only volunteer who shows up early these days."

Preston told Daniel where he'd be, then went back to the ranch's office. The door was partially open, so he didn't bother to knock.

Abby wasn't in the main room, so he went to the kitchen. What he saw blasted a hole through his gut. Abby was sitting at the table and crying softly.

"Abby, what's wrong?" he asked, pulling her into his arms.

"No one's supposed to see me like this," she said. Taking a breath, she stepped back and quickly wiped the tears from her face. "Didn't Bobby close the door?" She smiled. "No, of course he didn't, the little sneak. He went looking for you, didn't he?"

"He's a smart kid and he's totally loyal to you, as I am. Now tell me what happened."

"So he didn't tell you?"

"He said he'd promised you that he wouldn't."

Abby nodded, then with a trace of reluctance, told him what Stan had said. "It scares me, Preston, but I'm not going to sell the animals or the ranch. If I can't fix things here, that failure will hang over me like a cloud, and that'll keep me from ever getting the backing I'll need to start over. I have to make my stand here." She took a deep breath, then let it out slowly. "Sometimes you just have to go for it and be willing to accept the consequences if things don't pan out."

"No matter what it takes, I won't stop until the killer's behind bars," he said, tilting her head up and meeting her eyes. "You've got my word."

"I'll do all I can to help you," she said, straightening her shoulders. "No more falling apart."

He wanted to hold her but knew that wasn't what she needed from him right now. "Abby, you've got courage, but you need a little help. Remember when we spoke about fetishes?"

She nodded. "You said Falcon was wrong for me, but you knew the right one."

He reached into his pocket and brought out the small leather pouch. "Open it."

As she held the tiny carved figure of White Wolf, he saw her expression change from weary determination to fascination. She'd opened her heart to him, and now the beliefs that had always given him strength were helping her.

Somewhere along the way he'd fallen hard for Abby, and the connection between them was as real as the White Wolf fetish she held in her hands. Leaving her would tear him apart, but when the time came, he'd do what had to be done. He wouldn't allow the darkness of his world to cast its shadow over hers.

"It's so beautiful," she said softly. "Tell me more about Wolf."

"White Wolf. This fetish is for those who think with their hearts. She's all about loyalty, protectiveness, caring and love. She bestows insight."

"What an incredible, precious gift."

"White Wolf is now your spiritual sister. When you feel hemmed in by circumstances beyond your control, clear your mind and think about White Wolf, then see what ideas come to you."

"I will." She wrapped her arms around his neck and kissed him gently. "I'll carry this with me always, and every time I look at it, you'll be there in my thoughts."

Before he could answer, they both heard a light knock on the door. Turning, they saw Daniel walk in.

"I've got some bad news," he said, motioning them toward the door.

Chapter Twenty

As soon as they left her office, Daniel held out a small device in the palm of his hand. "We found a half dozen of these in the bunkhouse and the office. They're cheap RF models but effective. They're easily available, too, if you know where to look."

"RF?" Abby asked.

"Radio frequency. These are listening devices that send conversations to a radio receiver within range," Preston said.

"So I've been bugged. Can the person on the other end still hear us?" she asked in an almost whisper.

"No. I've disabled these," Daniel said, "but you might have more in your office and in the house. I'd like to check."

Her eyes widened. "Please do!"

Daniel went through her office, then her house. After he was done, he joined them and showed them the four small listening devices he'd found. "The two in the ranch office were on or around your desk. The ones in your home were on your portable phones."

"This would explain how our moves were second-guessed from the very beginning. I thought it was the reporter's fault, but I may have been wrong about that," Preston said.

"Kyle also found out something interesting about the painting by Whit McCabe," Daniel said. "While I was sweeping the buildings, Kyle used my computer and did a search. 'The Rodeo' disappeared ten years ago from a private collector's gallery. That's before Carl went to prison. It was insured for six figures. Selling something high profile like that to a legitimate gallery or collector would have been impossible, of course, and on the black market it would have only commanded a fraction of its worth."

"So maybe Carl was biding his time, looking for just the right buyer," Preston said.

"That doesn't sound like Carl, but I'll tell you what does—and this is something you need to keep in mind," Abby said. "If someone was keeping tabs on Carl, he would have known. Carl was always on his guard. He was the only person Bobby never could sneak up on."

"Maybe he found the bugs but left them in place, deliberately misleading whoever was listening in. Inmates learn a lot of survival skills in prison, so that makes sense," Preston said. "But here's something else—he didn't run. That tells me he wasn't afraid for his life. Carl may have had something he felt would keep his ex-partner at bay—leverage of sorts. He wasn't concerned when his killer came calling because he was counting on something else to protect him—a bargaining chip, information that could lead to a bigger payoff or penalty."

"Then why didn't he use it to save his life?" Abby asked.

"Remember that Carl was beaten to death. Rage often overwhelms logic," Preston said.

"So we're now looking for something else he hid in the office?" Abby asked.

"Yes, but this time it wouldn't be something he needed to safeguard in the same way he did the painting. We're talking information of some kind—notes, a letter, something his partner would have really wanted or feared. And it's bound to be in a place that's meant to be overlooked."

"Can I help?" Bobby asked.

Abby jumped and turned around quickly. "Bobby, I'm going to have to put a bell around your neck."

Preston smiled. "I knew you were there."

"Yeah, I know," Bobby said. "I saw you glance out of the corner of your eye. Spies do that."

Preston smiled. "You're good spotting little details, Bobby, so come along with us."

Daniel and Kyle followed Preston and Bobby into the barn and stopped to look through the open door of Carl's small office. Visible were a filing cabinet, an old desk and chair, an ancient rotary phone and a few shelves with business papers. "You're the one who has the eyes for things like this, Preston," Daniel said.

Preston nodded. "I'd like to focus on the ordinary at first, like floorboards that aren't flush, trim that's loose, gaps between objects. Concentrate on potential hiding places."

As they all started searching, Preston got down on the floor and worked his way slowly toward the old wooden desk. He was looking for changes in elevation, but as he shifted to one side, the bottom of Carl's chair caught his eye. There was a tiny slit in the cushion.

"I've got something, but it might just be a sign of wear on an old chair." He studied the slit at the inside end of the cushion. The diagonal cut disappeared beneath the back of the chair.

With Daniel's help, Preston loosened the metal post that held the two parts in place and removed the back rest, which slid into a metal bracket. The slit, easily visible now, was longer than he'd realized. Part of it had been hidden by the mechanism.

Preston reached inside with a gloved hand. "I've got something." A moment later he pulled out a small spiral notebook.

"Cool," Bobby said.

"Do you recognize Carl's writing?" he asked Bobby as he opened the notebook.

Bobby nodded.

Preston took a closer look at what was written inside. The first section, a total of maybe five pages, was easy to read, but then the words stopped and gave way to what was clearly a number-based code. "Can you make this out?" he asked Daniel.

He looked at it and expelled his breath in a hiss. "I've got some decryption programs I can run it through," he said. "It's probably some number-for-letter substitution code."

"Can I see?" Bobby asked.

When Preston showed it to him, Bobby smiled. "He and I came up with this code. We'd leave notes for each other, spy-craft, you know? I told you that when I meet my dad some-day—"

Preston stopped him gently. "*How* do you decode this?"

"Simple. The letter A is 26 and B is 25, all the way down to Z, which is one. So Bobby would be 25-12-25-25-2. Get it?"

"I'll program the decryption and it can translate the numbers automatically for us," Daniel said. He tried to use his smart phone but after a moment looked up. "I'm not getting a connection from here."

"That's why Carl used the old-school landline," Abby said. "Let's go to my office. You'll have a reliable Wi-Fi connection there."

Five minutes later Daniel had decoded the first section. "Here's a quick rundown of what I've got so far. Right before the police caught up to him, Carl had a falling-out with his partner. The guy discovered that Carl hadn't been splitting the take fifty-fifty and was out for blood, so once Carl left prison, he changed his name and went into hiding. Carl figured that one day the guy would track him down, so he kept a few things in reserve in case he needed money to run."

"So Carl hadn't really turned his life around," Abby said softly.

"Yes and no," Daniel said. "He wasn't a thief anymore, but

he also needed to survive. That took priority over returning what he'd taken."

"So who *was* his partner?" Preston asked.

"The journal never mentions anyone, including Carl himself by name. I'm guessing that was his way of remaining anonymous in case it was found prematurely."

"It also protected Bobby, too, in the off chance he might have found it during one of the games they played," Abby said. "Carl knew Bobby had a good eye." She looked over at Bobby, who nodded solemnly.

"There's a second part here, too, but it uses a different code entirely," Daniel said. "I'm guessing that section will reveal which pieces of art Carl held on to and maybe where he stashed them. My computer's trying to decrypt it now, but it may take time, depending on how complex the code is."

"I bet I can figure it out," Bobby said. "I know how Carl's brain worked. He and I used to play spy all the time and make up all kinds of ciphers. We'd pretend that we were CIA field officers and needed help from our agents," Bobby said. In a sad voice, he added, "I'll miss him."

Preston looked at Bobby for a second, then making up his mind, added, "Bobby, give me your cell phone."

He pulled it out of his pocket and turned it over to Preston.

Preston found the camera app, then, taking the notebook from Daniel, took photos of the relevant pages. "I'm trusting you with this, Bobby, but I need your word you won't tell *anyone* that you're helping the police. That has to be top secret. Will you agree to the terms?"

Bobby nodded. "Yeah, and you can trust me. Just ask Abby."

"I don't have to, I trust *you*."

Bobby beamed him a smile. "I'll crack it, probably faster than the computer because it didn't know Carl. To really solve a puzzle or break a code you need to think like the person who made it up. That's what Angus McAdams said in his book *Spycraft*. Of course, that's not the author's real name. He had to keep his real identity hidden."

Preston glanced at Abby, Daniel and Bobby. "The existence of this journal has to stay between us for now. That way there'll be zero chance that the information will be leaked to the press. As long as Carl's partner doesn't know we have this, we have the advantage."

"But Carl didn't give us any names," Abby said. "We have no way of identifying this person."

"Carl obviously committed most of his thefts in Denver and on the West Coast, but he may have started his life of crime here in Hartley. What if he formed his partnership here at the very beginning? None of the other investigators have been able to find that person, but maybe they've been looking in the wrong place," Preston said. "The first thing we need to do is find out who Carl's associates were before he left for the big city and track their movements. Perhaps one of them has recently moved back here, from Denver or one of the other cities where Carl operated."

"You're looking for an old buddy of Carl's, maybe a criminal who never got caught?" Abby said.

Bobby looked at them. "You should talk to Mrs. Whitcomb. She came to our school to tell us about the old days. She's lived here forever, and Mr. Whitcomb was a famous lawman. He was the only sheriff around for like a hundred miles."

"Sadie Whitcomb—I know her," Abby said. "She doesn't have a lot of money, but once a month, like clockwork, she sends us a small check. I'm sure she'll help us." Abby smiled. "But I should warn you she's quite a character. Unless she knows you, she won't open her door. She'll just pretend she's not home. She's close to a hundred so you won't be able to use your badge to push her either."

"How's her memory?" Preston asked.

"For what happened two days ago, not so good, but forty years ago, that's like yesterday. She can remember details that'll amaze you. I invite her to the ranch from time to time so she can look around and have some fun. She's just amazing."

"Where does she live?"

"Down the same road as Meadow Park."

"The retirement community? That's about ten miles from here," Preston confirmed. "Let's go."

As they left the office and walked to his SUV, Preston glanced off in the direction of the barns. "Ilse sure gets around."

Abby saw Ilse laugh and then give Stan a quick kiss. "Don't see too much in that. Ilse likes men and she's single," she said and shrugged. "Deep down she's got a good heart. She volunteers here a lot."

Preston watched them for a second longer, then climbed into his SUV. "They look like old friends having fun."

"They probably are friends. Both of them spend a lot of time working here."

Preston followed Abby's directions to a small *casita* surrounded by fruit trees a quarter mile off the main highway. A chain-link fence bordered the property. The small front yard, probably a lawn at one time, was mostly gravel now. Two cats were watching them from a bench atop the small porch.

Abby led the way, but as they stepped onto the porch, Sadie opened the door. "I saw you pull up, Abby. Did you come for a donation? I read in the paper about all the troubles you've been having."

Sadie invited them to take a seat on the sofa and after hearing what they wanted, she nodded. "I can help you. I knew Carl Sinclair when he was just a kid, and even back then I can tell you he was always up to no good." She looked directly at Abby. "I'm so sorry that I never took a closer look at Carl Woods. If I had, I could have warned you, Abby."

"It wasn't your fault. I knew about his past, but I believed him when he told me he'd changed," Abby said.

"His kind doesn't change," she said, leaning back in her chair. "My husband, Jeremiah, was the county sheriff back then, and he kept a close eye on troublemakers like Carl."

"Did he ever actually arrest him?" Abby asked.

"No, he never could get anything on him or his buddy, another troublemaker Jeremiah couldn't abide. When several Whit McCabe paintings were stolen from a collector here in town, Jeremiah was sure Carl and his friend were responsible because Carl had worked for the man at one time. Jeremiah tried hard to find something to tie them to the theft but couldn't. Then the owner of the stolen paintings passed on, and his son wasn't interested in art. He settled for the insurance money and auctioned off the rest of his dad's collection. There weren't any other suspects, so I think the insurance company stopped looking after that."

"Did your husband ever mention Carl's partner by name?" Preston asked.

"All I remember is that Jeremiah called him 'The Liquidator.' From the bits and pieces he told me about, the man dealt in stolen property, but he also knew how to cover his tracks. He never flaunted his wealth, and when he wasn't traveling, he spent his time at a small cabin just this side of Navajo Dam," she said. "He died in a hunting accident a few years before my husband passed. Guess he didn't have any living relatives because no one ever claimed the body." She paused. "Come to think of it, his cabin is probably still up there above the lake. I suppose you could go take a look."

"Do you know where it is?" Preston asked.

"Only that it's northwest of Navajo Dam, off the main road. Jeremiah mentioned that you had to go past a cliff with two large rocks that looked like fangs at its base. There was a gully and a dirt road that led up the hill. You couldn't see the cabin from the highway, I recall him saying."

"I'm not sure if that's going to be enough to find the place," Abby said.

"I camped out in that area when I was in high school, and we drove up that highway a dozen or more times. Believe it or not, I know the cliff that she referred to. *Hosteen* Silver said they were *Tsé Íí'áhí,* like the two Churchrock Spires east of Gallup," Preston said.

"Spires, I get, but I don't speak Navajo, dear," Sadie said. "What does that word mean in English?"

"Sorry, ma'am. Loosely, it means 'standing rock,'" he said, turning to Abby and nodding. "If those rocks are still within sight of the road, we'll find them."

Chapter Twenty-One

The drive took them through the town of Bloomfield, then past the small community of Blanco. Preston kept glancing in the rearview mirror.

"Hang on," he said, then suddenly braked hard and took a sharp left down a farm road.

Abby hung on to the door handle to balance herself in her seat. "What are you doing? We're not even close to the dam!"

"There was a dark green vehicle back there. He was hanging way back, so I'm not really sure it was a tail, but I saw it after we left Sadie's." Preston stopped and looked back into the mirror again. "He's gone now."

"So what do we do now?"

"Wait five minutes, then continue our drive. Keep a watch for green vehicles parked by the highway, in case he's hoping to pick us up again," Preston said. "I couldn't really tell if it was a van or an SUV, but I am sure of the color."

Eventually they got back on the road, crossed the massive rock and earthen dam and entered the pine-covered hills above, leaving the big canyon behind. They drove along the highway just under the speed limit, not wanting to miss any of the landmarks. Preston took a wide curve, and off to their left he spotted the low sandstone cliff with the two rocks at the bottom.

"Tsé Íi'áhí." Preston nodded in that direction. "Smaller than I remember, though."

"Pointy and like fangs," Abby said. "Sadie was right."

They continued around the long curve and as they rounded the bend, he saw a dark green SUV pulling off the shoulder and onto the highway. It passed by, heading in the opposite direction. The driver had his head turned away, and Preston couldn't get a clear look.

"Is that the same SUV you saw before?" she asked.

"I'm not sure," he said.

With no oncoming cars, he was able to do a one-eighty on the highway and parked along the shoulder where the SUV had been moments earlier. A three-wire cattle fence was in place on both sides of the road.

"The ground is soft, and it won't be an easy hike, but it looks like we have to walk from here," Preston said.

"Good thing I'm wearing boots," she said.

They'd hiked about twenty feet up the wash when Preston noticed something on the ground up ahead. "Footprints. Maybe the person in the van came this way, too."

"Call of nature?" Abby asked.

He sniffed the air and glanced around. "Naw, I smell… gasoline?" Up ahead he saw a thin curl of black smoke rising into the air just around the curve of the arroyo.

"Campfire?"

"Not with gasoline," he said and handed Abby his keys. "Go back and get the fire extinguisher out of my unit. Hurry."

As Preston raced up the slope, he noticed the increasingly strong smell of burning wood and gasoline. About a hundred feet up, the ground evened out and Preston saw an old, sturdy-looking log cabin about fifty feet ahead. Its roof was mostly intact, but one side of the cabin was on fire with flames shooting out about two feet into the air.

Preston looked around for something to use to fight the

fire and saw a gallon-size metal can on the ground, like from a cafeteria kitchen. He'd use that to scoop up wet sand from the wash and maybe slow down the fire until Abby returned.

The can reeked of gasoline; the container probably was left by the arsonist after he'd siphoned fuel from his SUV. Needing to work quickly before the fire ignited the surrounding forest, Preston used it to dig out some wet sand from the wash and throw that onto the base of the flames.

It seemed to help. Or maybe the logs were so wet from recent rains they didn't want to burn. He quickly scooped up more sand and threw it against the base of the flames. The fire died some, and the hole he was digging in the wash was now filling with water. There was hope.

Two minutes later, he saw Abby come over the rise, fire extinguisher in hand. "This is heavy," she yelled, running up.

"Let's trade," he said, holding out the can.

"After all my running uphill?" she said, pulling the safety pin on the extinguisher. "No way. Give me some room."

Within twenty seconds, Abby had put out the flames. "Shall I work it over some more?" she asked, coughing from the smoke of still-smoldering wood.

"I reached water level in the wash," Preston said. "Stand by. I'll flood it."

Five minutes later the wall, nearly soaked with muddy water, was still intact.

"We use cans like that to scoop out grain at the ranch. I don't suppose you'll be able to get fingerprints from it now, right?" she asked.

"I've obliterated them with the wet sand, water and my own prints, but I had to slow the fire down."

"You think the person in the SUV did this?"

"Almost certainly," Preston answered. "Did you happen to get a look at the driver's face?"

"No, I was looking around for the cabin," she said, then

glanced back at the small building. "Do you think we'll find any of the answers we need here?"

"You never know." Preston looked at the small porch. "The door is sturdy and there's a rusted padlock in place, protected by the hasp. Let me see if there's any sign of a break-in."

They circled the cabin, but the windows, boarded over, hadn't been broached and the structure itself looked intact.

"Did you happen to notice the tire ruts in the back?" Preston asked. "There's a road back here somewhere, but I'm guessing the guy in the SUV couldn't figure out where it was."

"So now that we're here, how do we get inside the cabin?"

Preston smiled. "I have some skills, but look away. It's better if you don't actually see what I'm about to do." He reached into his jacket pocket for the special lock picks he kept in case of an emergency.

Soon they were inside, looking around the two-room cabin. Dust and cobwebs covered everything. "No one's been inside for months—years maybe," he said.

"The dresser drawers have some men's clothing, but it's old and threadbare." Abby went to the bookcase next. The books, mostly paperbacks, were yellow and dried up. The newest book was from 1995.

Preston picked up a small picture frame from a simple wooden desk. "I think this is Carl," he said, looking at the faded photo.

Abby came over to take a closer look. "He looks much younger in this photo, of course, but it's him. From the way they're dressed and the haircuts, I think it was taken in the mid-sixties. I don't know the man with him. Do you?"

Preston shook his head. "Maybe the owner of the cabin? I'll run a special facial-recognition program and find out."

"What if he doesn't have a criminal record?"

"If he ever applied for a driver's license or had VA papers, my brother's computer will ID him. That's why I'm going to ask him to do it. He has fewer rules and regulations to worry about."

"Jealous?" she asked and smiled.

He met her gaze and held it. "Abby, you probably won't believe this but, no, I'm not jealous. I've always played things by the book."

"What's changed?"

"You're more important to me than any rule book," he said, then took her hand and brushed a kiss over her knuckles. "We're making progress on this case, Abby, so it won't be long before you have your life back."

She wanted to ask if he'd still be a part of it but remained silent. She had him here with her today. She wouldn't ask him for more than he could give.

THEY WERE BACK in Hartley, in Daniel's kitchen nook sipping hot coffee, when Dan called them across to his work area.

"It took longer than I expected, but I've got an ID for you. The man in the photo is Miles Gates," he said.

"The name's not familiar to me," Preston said.

"According to court records, thirty or so years ago Gates was the local go-to guy if you wanted high-end art stolen. He never did the job himself. He provided intel and support. Like Carl, he lived in the Four Corners area most of his life."

"The photo tells us that they were friends, or at least colleagues, but if he's passed on, the trail ends there," Abby said. "There's no one else in the photo."

Preston stood silently, staring at an indeterminate point across the room. "I need to find someone who's connected to those two men. Carl had no family, but maybe Gates did."

Preston sat by the computer and got to work. As the minutes ticked by, no one interrupted him.

"Stan Cooper," he said at last. "That's the link."

"Stan? If you think he has anything to do with the problems I've had or with Carl's death, you're way off the mark. When I first opened the ranch, bookkeeping was nearly my downfall. Stan stepped up and took over—pro bono. He also introduced me to people like Rod Garner. Both of those men have been crucial to the ranch's operations. Stan's one of the good guys."

Preston shook his head. "Stan's grandmother remarried late in life. She was Miles's wife. He'd told me before that he'd spent a lot of time in the area around Navajo Dam, but I didn't have enough to put things together then."

"You can't hold Stan responsible for something his relative did," Abby said.

"No, but Stan's the common denominator. Here's my theory. Stan either remembered Carl or did some checking up and somehow confirmed his identity. Then maybe he tried to shake Carl down and pressure him to give up the missing paintings. Something went wrong and it led to Carl's death."

"You have nothing, bro," Daniel said.

"Abby, tell me what you know about Stan and Ilse," Preston said.

"I'd never seen her fooling around with Stan until today."

Preston paced, lost in thought. "Here's something we hadn't considered. What if the thing she supposedly had with Monroe was only a smokescreen? She came on heavily to the kid the night Carl was killed, but it might have been a way to keep him busy while Stan dealt with Carl."

"You're seeing way too much in this," Abby said. "Ilse's a free spirit. I may not agree with the things she does, but she doesn't have to answer to anyone but herself. Her life's her own."

"I'm not convinced, but obviously I need to find a stronger connection between those two. That means I'm going to need to dig deeper into Ilse's past. She's more of an unknown."

"I ran a full background on her," Daniel said. "No warrants, no arrests. If there had been any flags whatsoever, I would have found them."

"Go further back, to her college days. Remember the disciplinary action?" Preston said.

"Her official record didn't specify any of the details, but I can hack into the college's computer."

"Do it."

Several minutes later Daniel looked up. "It's sketchy, but she apparently put a bug in the math instructor's office, then tried to blackmail her."

"Like the listening devices at the ranch?" Abby said. "But Ilse's college days are long behind her. So she sowed some wild oats back then, so what?"

"It establishes an M.O.," Preston said. "What if Ilse found out about Carl? Garner said Carl told him the truth about his past, so if Ilse had been listening in when he did, she would have known. It's possible she told Stan after that and they joined forces."

"Rod does careful background checks on everyone in his circle. His former assistant handled Ilse's, but Ilse would have been the one responsible for running a check on Stan. Maybe that's when she made the connection," Abby said.

Preston expelled his breath in a hiss. "It's all plausible, and even likely, but it's just a bedtime story unless we find proof."

"How do we do that?" Abby asked.

Preston remained quiet, then after a beat looked up. "We get creative and work fast."

Chapter Twenty-Two

"Here's the way I see it," Preston said. "We'll need to sweep Garner's office, but there's a problem. The minute I tell him why I want to do that, he might toss me out on my ear and handle the problem himself."

"I can help you there," Abby said. "If Ilse and Stan have been working against me, I need to know, and to hold up in court, the search would have to be done right. Rod loves the ranch so I'm sure I can persuade him to give us his permission."

"Obviously you'll have to do that when Ilse isn't there, so you have to time your request right," Daniel said. "And I shouldn't be part of this. You'll want Garner to stay calm and that'll work better if he's around people he knows."

"Let me call Rod now. I know how I have to handle this." Abby reached for her cell phone and a moment later Ilse put her through. "Rod, I need a huge favor. Do you have time for me today?" she asked a beat later.

"For you—always," he replied. "What can I do for you?"

"It's something I'd rather not talk about over the phone. Okay if I come over?"

"Sure, when should I expect you?"

"How about in twenty minutes, say, five-thirty? I know Ilse leaves around five. Is that too late?"

"Nah, just come over. You've got me curious now."

They were on their way in Preston's SUV a short time later. "It's really important that you don't discuss the case until *after* I sweep Garner's place," Preston said.

"No problem," Abby said with a nod. "Just follow my lead, and don't let it throw you if he loses his cool. The best way to respond is don't react in kind."

"I gather you've seen him at his worst?"

She nodded. "Rod's hot-tempered. I was there one time when Ilse forgot to book his tickets to an NBA game he wanted to attend. When he goes crazy like he did that day, he can be hard to deal with."

"Does he get violent?" Preston asked her.

"Not in the way you think. He doesn't attack anyone, but I've seen him hurl things across his office and smash stuff against the wall. He won't deliberately aim at anyone, but be ready to duck anyway."

Preston's jaw clenched.

She glanced at him. "I mean it—don't let it get you upset. Just stay calm."

"Got it."

WHEN THEY ARRIVED at Rod's home, they were shown in by the butler. The second they stepped into the den, Rod looked at Preston, then back at Abby. "Didn't know you were bringing the law. I'm not going to like this visit, am I?"

"I was hoping that you could show the detective your gym and basketball court. The department may do a special fundraiser for us," she said. "Maybe have the police versus the fire department or something like that."

"Sure, come on," Rod said, instantly in a brighter mood. "Count me in on whatever you plan to do, too. I'll be happy to help."

They left Rod's office and went outside, crossing the lawn to another building.

"Rod, before we go any further—I haven't been entirely honest with you," Abby said, stopping and turning to look at him.

Rod glared at Preston instead of Abby. "What kind of game do you have my girl playing?"

"No, listen," Abby insisted, forcing him to look back at her. "I'm trying to protect you."

Hearing the words made him react in exactly the way she'd hoped. "Little girl, whatcha talking about?" he asked with a grin.

"Ilse may not be the person you think she is," Abby said. "I really hope I'm wrong, but we've found some bugs in and around Carl's office and the bunkhouse. A few were in my house, too. Because of Ilse's past, we have reason to suspect she's responsible."

"You think Ilse's been spying on people—and on me?" Rod said, an edge of steel in his voice.

"Which is why we needed to get you outside. We don't know anything for sure, but isn't it worth finding out?" Abby asked him, making sure to keep her voice soft and calm.

"That's why you're here?" he asked, looking at Preston.

"I brought some special equipment that'll tell us for sure if your place is bugged."

"Let's go."

Abby recognized the angry gleam in Rod's eye and the set of his jaw as they walked toward Preston's SUV.

"Rod, are you okay?" she asked.

"Yeah, but Ilse and I are going to war if I find out she's been bugging my office. That's *not* cool," he said through clenched teeth.

ABBY AND ROD stood in the doorway, far back as Preston swept Garner's office with methodical precision. The first bug he found was right underneath the big man's desk. He held it up for them to see.

Before Rod could react, Abby pulled him out through French doors and onto the patio.

Rod instantly picked up a vase filled with flowers and threw it against the wall. Water trickled down the wall and flowers scattered all over the tile floor. Rod paced like a caged tiger. "She was going to sell me out, wasn't she?"

"Rod, easy. Anger won't solve anything."

"Oh yeah, it will. Next time she shows up she's going to find out why no one messes with me."

Preston came outside and held up three electronic monitoring devices in two separate packs. "They're not transmitting, so you can speak freely," he said. "Assuming she didn't also bug the patio."

Preston checked but found nothing.

"I owe you one, guy, and I always pay my debts, as Ilse is about to find out," Rod said.

"Play it smart by playing her. It'll get you a lot further," Preston said. "Ilse handled the background checks on people in your circle, right?"

"Yeah, man. A guy in my position has to be careful. Everybody's a user and a con artist these days. I had my people run a check on her, too, and she was clean."

"Yes, she was—back then. Now she's involved in something that's illegal. Any idea why? Does she have any money problems?"

"I have no idea," he said with a shrug, "but if you let me handle this my way, I guarantee I'll get answers."

Preston shook his head. "I believe Ilse may have played a part in Carl's murder and I need the kind of evidence that'll stand up in court. The best thing you can do right now is give me permission to search her work area. Are you okay with that?"

"Sure. Do whatever you need. Nail her hide to the wall," Rod said.

Abby kept Rod outside as Preston began to search. "Are you sure you're going to be okay? Is it possible she managed to get something that might be embarrassing to you?"

He laughed. "Honey, these days I lead a downright boring life. During my days playing pro ball, well, that was a different story."

"Do you remember where you were when Carl first told you who he was?" Preston asked him, coming back out.

"Yeah, my office, having iced tea. We'd just played some pick-up ball out on my court." He pressed his lips tightly. "Ilse set him up, didn't she?" he said in a low growl.

"We don't know anything for sure yet, but that's the way it looks to me," Preston said. "Let me check around some more."

After about twenty minutes Preston called them into Ilse's office. "I found two unused burn phones, one taped beneath a drawer, an RF receiver disguised as an MP3 player and earphones. She was monitoring your conversations both on the phone and off. Ilse is in this up to her neck."

"Arrest her," Rod said, storming around the office. "I'll press charges. And I'll sue her, too. I want life as she knows it to be *over*. Carl was a friend of mine. If she set him up, she pays," he said, striding around the room. "That man trusted *me* and that trust was violated here in my own home. No way she's getting away with that."

He picked up Ilse's coffee cup and threw it on the floor, shattering it into a dozen pieces. "I'm pitching her out to the curb with the rest of the trash." He kicked away Ilse's desk chair, and it flew across the room and bounced off the wainscoting.

"Seeing her behind bars is your best revenge, but you need to play *her*, remember? Stay cool, and don't tip our hand,"

Preston said. "Once I gather more evidence I'll take her down."

Rod stopped pacing and looked Preston in the eye. "Okay, I've got that out of my system. What do you need?"

"Information. Does Ilse have a car?"

"Not her own, no. The SUV she drives belongs to Garner Inc.," Rod said. "What are you after?"

"I'd like to track her whereabouts the night of Carl's murder," Preston said.

"Easy. The SUV's got a GPS," he said. "I'll get you the chip. It'll tell you everywhere the SUV's been, along with the dates and times. It's *my* wheels, so you don't have to worry about a warrant. You've got my permission to access anything you need."

"I'll give you a receipt for it, and once we've copied the data, you can have it back."

"Let's go. The SUV she drives is the green one that's parked in front of the garage. It'll only take me a few minutes to pull the chip. I do this every year for my accountant—tax deductions, you know."

Preston looked at his watch. "Is there a chance Ilse will need the SUV and catch on?"

He glanced out the back window. "Ilse lives in that *casita*," he said, pointing. "The glow through the curtains is from her 40-inch TV. That tells us that she's viewing her favorite TV show, which she records on her DVR. She watches it religiously as soon as her workday is over. For the next hour or so, she'll stay put."

Five minutes later, memory card in hand, Preston went back to his SUV and called the station. After speaking to the IT tech, he uploaded the GPS data via his MDT. Before long, he had the information he needed in a clear printout.

Preston went back to the house and met with Abby and Rod. "Ilse was up by Navajo Dam," he told Abby but didn't fill in the details for Rod. "More important, she went to the bus station a few hours after Carl's death."

"No way Ilse would travel by bus. That chick's high maintenance. She rents a car if she goes out of town on private business."

"Well, considering she's still around and didn't take any trips, I suspect she stored something in one of the lockers there," Preston said.

"Okay, B-man, what's next? Can you get a warrant and search the lockers?" Rod asked.

"No, just the ones she's using, and we'd have to specify what we're looking for. Since we don't know the answers to either of those questions, we can't make a move. Right now all I can get her for is misdemeanor invasion of privacy. To get her for anything more, we need to handle it differently. First, I'll need to put all the bugs I found in your office back where they were."

"Say again?"

"You heard me," Preston said. "We don't want to tip her off. What we need to do is set her up by having her overhear a staged conversation. I'll make sure it rattles her enough to force her into making a mistake."

"I don't know about that," Rod said. "Ilse doesn't rattle easily. That's one of the reasons I hired her. Even when I lose my cool, she barely blinks."

"Speaking of that, make sure you replace that broken cup in her office, and maybe the vase on the patio. When she comes back here, it has to look as if nothing out of the ordinary happened."

"You bet," Rod said. "How long do you need to set everything up?"

"Till morning. When does she get to her desk?"

"Eight-thirty," Rod said. "Unless something special is coming up, Ilse keeps regular hours."

"We'll set things in motion then. Just play along with whatever I say."

"You've got it."

After leaving Garner's estate, Preston drove toward Daniel's place, where he arranged to meet his brothers.

They arrived fifteen minutes later. Preston waited as the heavy metal gate opened so he could drive through. "This is going to be an all-nighter, Abby. You sure you want in? I can take you home right now."

"Michelle is going to be with the animals, so I'm staying. Everything I value is on the line." Even as she said it, she realized how true that was. And there was more than her beloved ranch at risk. Standing with her in the thick of things was the man she'd learned to love.

THEY'D ALL CATNAPPED a few hours on the sofas in Daniel's sitting area, but it was close to daylight by the time they went over the details one last time.

"Everyone know what to do?" Preston's gaze took them all in, one at a time—Abby, Daniel, Kyle and Gene. Once everyone nodded, they stood.

"Let's grab something to eat, then get back to the ranch," Preston said. "From this moment on, we keep things as routine as possible."

ABBY SPENT THE next two hours tending the animals. She was getting ready to return to Rod's place when she saw Bobby's foster dad pull up.

"In all the confusion, I totally forgot that I'd promised Bobby he could stay here this weekend!" she said, thumping her forehead with the heel of her hand.

Preston shook his head. "Don't make a big deal out of it. Kyle should be here any minute. He can watch over Bobby while he's guarding the ranch." He gestured toward the gate as he finished speaking. "There he is now."

Preston hurried to meet Kyle. "Hey, bro, one more favor."

"Dude, what'll you ever do without me once I'm gone?"

"I'll try to bear up," Preston said, biting back a grin. "Now listen up. We need you to watch over Bobby while you're here. In another thirty minutes, if it goes according to plan, things are going to get heavy."

"You hope," Kyle said.

"My plans don't fail," Preston said.

Preston then called the station and verified that a patrolman was in position and keeping an eye on the guest house inside Garner's estate. The officer was to report in if Ilse returned there any time during the day.

Then Preston joined Abby. "Ready?"

"Whenever you are."

As they got under way, Abby listened as Preston went over their plans one more time. If Preston was right, and Ilse and Stan were behind Carl's murder, the case would be solved soon. After that Preston would go back to his life and get involved in another case, and what they'd shared would soon become just another memory. She swallowed hard at the bittersweet prospects ahead.

"Hopefully this will all be over for you soon, and you'll be able to pick up your life right where you left off."

She shook her head. "I can never go back to the way things were. I've learned too much about myself. The ranch will always be at the center of my life, but I don't want it to be my entire world. I want…more."

He nodded slowly. "You deserve the best of everything, Abby."

"After the case is closed, will you still come to visit?" She hadn't meant to voice it out loud, but now that she had, she didn't regret it. She needed to hear his answer.

"I wish the answer could be yes, but I'm not the man you need beside you, Abby." He tightened his grip on the wheel until his knuckles turned white. "Our worlds would collide and eventually destroy one or both of us. A cop's work is filled with long shadows, the kind that follow a man after he quits for the day. You need to focus on hope and optimism. That's the heart of everything Sitting Tall Ranch does."

"Shadows have always been part of my life, Preston, and I've never hidden from them. I face them, then try to push them back, at least temporarily, for the kids." She paused. "The real problem between us is that you don't trust love and, without that, no relationship can survive."

He looked at her for a moment. "I admit there's some truth to that—" Before he could go on, he got a text message from Rod. "Here we go. Ilse's at work now," Preston said, reading it. "Time for us to get things rolling. You ready?"

"Absolutely," she said.

As eager as she was for closure, she knew that saying goodbye to Preston would follow, and nothing she could do, or say, would protect her from the heartbreak to come.

Chapter Twenty-Three

As they walked inside Rod's home, Abby noticed that things looked perfectly ordinary again, including the patio, visible through the French doors. A moment later Ilse, with her usual smile, escorted them down a short hall into Rod's office.

As Ilse left the room and the door shut, they sat down. Rod gave Preston a thumbs-up.

"So what brings you here?" Rod asked, getting things started.

"After this case is closed, Sitting Tall Ranch will be in need of funds," she said.

"Some of the investments Stan made for me took another wrong turn so I've got some cash flow problems right now," he said. "But I'll be happy to help you with some fundraisers. You could hold some special event here on the estate and charge admission."

"I plan to get the department involved and maybe other city agencies," Preston said. "Of course, we'll have to wait until the case is closed, but it shouldn't be much longer now."

"What's changed?" Rod asked, instantly picking up his cue.

"We've found Carl Sinclair's journal. It's a police matter, so I can't really discuss it, but I can tell you this—although he wrote it in code, we've already cracked the first part and expect to have it all before the end of the day. We have reason to believe the journal holds the name of the man who came after him and the location of several stolen paintings Carl kept in hiding."

"So it's all over but the crying," Rod said. "Outstanding."

"I believe that by noon, midafternoon tops, we'll be ready to make some arrests," Preston said.

There was a soft knock on the door and Ilse came in. "I'm feeling a little under the weather, Rod, so unless you need me, I'd like to head home."

"That's fine. Go ahead," Rod said.

After Ilse left the office, Preston held a finger to his lips, reminding them that the bugs were still in place.

A few minutes later the three of them went outside onto the patio. Preston's phone rang. It was the patrolman who was watching the *casita* and Ilse.

"The subject's inside the house, Detective. Currently, she's on the phone. I can see her walking around."

"If she leaves, call me immediately."

"Copy."

About ten minutes later, as Preston and Abby were leaving the estate with Preston driving, they spotted a familiar-looking figure on the sidewalk down the street. Though carrying a large tote and wearing a hoodie and sweatpants, a far cry from her designer clothing, the woman's long-legged strides and purposeful walk gave her away.

"Don't look at her," Preston said. "We'll circle the block and come back around."

Preston called the patrolman as soon as he turned away. "She's not there, is she?"

"I haven't seen her for the past several minutes. She came to the window, looked around and then left the front room. Let me go in for a closer look."

Preston parked at the curb and waited. A few minutes later the officer called him. "She's gone, sir. She must have slipped out the back."

As Preston hung up, Abby looked over. "From the way she's walking, she's got a specific destination in mind."

He pulled out into traffic, then circled the block and cruised down the street. After a short distance, they spotted her again, walking down a graveled pathway among the grass and trees.

"She's cutting across the city park," Preston said. "I won't be able to follow her in the car. I'll have to park somewhere and go after her on foot."

"I'm going with you."

"No. Drive back to the ranch and wait for me." He took off his jacket, turned it inside out to change its color, then put it back on.

"Handy—a reversible jacket," Abby said. She quickly pulled her hair back into a ponytail and fastened it with a rubber band she had inside her purse. "I'm going with you. You're not the only one who wants to know what Ilse's up to."

"All right," he snapped, reaching for the Stetson in the backseat. "I don't have time to argue."

They climbed out of the SUV, leaving it parked at the curb, and started down the same path Ilse had chosen. They remained at a distance, screening themselves whenever possible with the natural contours of the ground, trees and bushes.

Preston kept his eye on Ilse but had to hold Abby back. "The key to tailing a suspect is patience and positioning. Keep them in sight, but always give them plenty of room. We look a little different now, but we still need to maintain our spacing."

"She's going to get away if we don't hurry up," Abby said, urging him on.

"No, she won't. She's headed for the bus station. She took the shortcut across the park because it knocks a couple of miles off her route and she can't be easily spotted by an officer in a police cruiser."

Although there had been no indication that Ilse suspected

they were there, she suddenly stopped, turned around and slowly searched the area behind her for followers.

Preston instantly stepped into the shadows of a tall pine tree, pulling Abby with him. Facing away from Ilse, he pressed Abby's back to the trunk of the tree and kissed her.

For one breathtaking moment, she forgot everything but Preston. His mouth was hard and insistent, and as she parted her lips he groaned and deepened the kiss.

Seconds later, he pulled back. The fire she saw in his eyes made a shiver course up her spine. He held her gaze for a brief eternity, then turned his head and looked across the park.

"She's on the move again. Time to go," he said. "Ilse's not taking anything for granted, and she's watching her back. Be ready for her to make more abrupt stops."

As they continued to tail Ilse, the memory of Preston's kiss burned inside Abby. She could still taste him and feel him against her. She loved him. No one had ever filled her with such strong longings, but Preston would never allow himself to need anyone other than his brothers.

The knowledge stung. With effort she forced herself to concentrate on Ilse. This woman was probably the key to catching Carl's killer and ending the case that threatened the ranch's continued existence. Ilse was the priority now.

As Ilse entered the bus depot, they waited a moment, then stepped inside and sat in an area where travelers were waiting with luggage and backpacks. Preston picked up an abandoned newspaper and handed Abby a section.

Ilse walked toward the ticket counter, then stopped to look around. They lowered their heads, pretending to read.

Ilse waited in the short line, bought a ticket, then stepped away, turning around again to make sure she wasn't followed. At long last, she walked toward the rear wall of the main floor and to the long row of metal lockers.

After one last look around, Ilse fished a key out of her tote and went to one of the larger storage units. She had a problem opening it, but after a moment, they saw her remove one medium-size cardboard mailing tube from the locker. She quickly tucked it under her arm, then started walking around as if bored and impatient.

"Got it," Preston said, lowering the cell phone he'd used to video Ilse's activity. "But if we move in now and that doesn't hold a stolen painting, she'll know for sure that we're on to her, and we'll never get the evidence we need. Let's stay back and watch her for a while longer."

Preston caught the eye of the plainclothes officer who'd been positioned to back him up and held up his hand, signaling him to wait.

"What if she jumps on the next bus? She has a ticket. She might even make an exchange as she wanders around through the crowd and we'll never see it happen."

"I've got that covered. She's on depot surveillance and has two sets of eyes on her. If she makes a move for the loading area outside, I'm arresting her. Trust me—I do this for a living."

Ilse suddenly turned and moved toward the loading zone door labeled Gate 1.

"Stay here, Abby," Preston said. He rose and nodded to the officer, who'd been standing across the room. The plainclothes cop moved over to cut Ilse off. Ilse, who was already on her guard, veered away, picking up speed as she headed for the Gate 2 door instead.

Preston had anticipated the move and was already blocking her way. The minute she saw him, she turned back but soon spotted the other officer.

"Ilse, stop. You're under arrest," Preston said.

Panicking, she looked toward the station entrance.

"Don't try it, Ilse. You'll never make it outside. If you resist, you'll only be making things worse for yourself," Preston said. "You're already facing serious charges."

The crowd of travelers, suddenly aware of what was going on, froze and stared silently as he cuffed Ilse's hands behind her back and informed her of her rights.

"Hang on to the lady, Detective Edwards," Preston said to the plainclothes officer.

As people started to talk and move around again, suspecting the action was over, Preston turned to go talk to Abby, but she wasn't where he'd left her. "The woman I came in with— where did she go?" he asked Edwards.

"Near the entrance talking to the guy in the sports jacket," Edwards replied with a directional nod of his head.

Preston turned, worked his way through the active crowd and saw Stan. They were near the main entrance—Stan holding Abby's forearm in a viselike grip. As Stan's eyes met his, Preston inched his hand down toward his gun.

Stan shook his head and moved back the lapel of his own jacket, revealing the handgun jammed into his waistband. For emphasis, he put his hand down on the butt.

Gesturing by cocking his head, Stan motioned for Preston to approach.

"What the hell?" Edwards muttered, coming up beside Preston, Ilse in tow.

"She's been taken hostage. Just hold on to the suspect. I've got this," Preston said, trying to keep his voice normal and not alarm bystanders. Any increase in the level of tension could get Abby shot.

As Preston drew near, Stan pulled Abby closer to him. "Lead the way outside, Bowman," he ordered. "Don't create a problem for Abby."

Preston opened the door and paused in the entry, looking back at them.

"Keep moving," Stan ordered. "Walk down the alley to the gas meter, then stop."

Preston saw Edwards start to advance. He held up his hand, halting the detective, and shook his head.

Fifteen seconds later, thirty feet down the alley, Preston stopped. "This is as far as we're going, Stan. We're going to be followed, you know that. Save yourself some jail time. Let Abby go and surrender your weapon."

"Not going to happen. I've got the hostage and I'm making the rules. Follow my instructions to the letter, Detective, or your woman will die. Am I clear?" Stan had his gun out and aimed at Abby's side.

"Yeah," Preston growled.

"Take out your weapon with your left hand *slowly,* then put it on the ground and slide it over to me with your foot," Stan said.

Preston put it on the ground as instructed, but he didn't kick it over. "You'll have to come get it. I've got it set for a one-pound trigger pull, and if I bump it too hard it could go off. A ricochet inside this alley could take any one of us down."

It was only a half-truth, but for now he hoped it would keep Stan from getting an additional weapon.

"You've been made, Stan, and Detective Edwards is already calling for backup," Preston added. "You've hit the end of the road in this alley. Let's make a deal before you have to face down a SWAT team."

Stan shook his head. "Catch." He tossed Preston a set of keys. "Once we get to the end my pickup's parked on the right. You'll drive and Abby and I will stay in the rear of the cab. If you try anything, I swear I'll shoot her in the head." He waved his gun slightly for emphasis.

Stan instructed them at gunpoint to walk to the end of the alley, where his truck was parked against the curb.

"Get in. It's unlocked," Stan ordered Preston.

"I've got Ilse and you've got Abby. Let's trade. That's what you want, right?"

"Not even close. Ilse knew the risks. She messed up, but I have no intention of making the same mistake." He poked the barrel of his pistol in Abby's side. "Now get in."

Preston had no other option at the moment. Stan's hand was shaking, and he couldn't risk Abby's life. He'd get his chance later, after they reached their destination. The department would also be tracking his cell phone. They wouldn't be alone for long.

He climbed into the driver's seat, looking back as Abby and then Stan slid into the car. At the far end of the alley, he could see Detective Edwards standing there, phone to his ear.

"Face forward, start up and drive. Don't look back again unless you want to hear gunfire."

"Where are we going?" Preston asked, inserting the key.

"Pull out into traffic and head west. You'll find out soon enough," Stan said. "One more thing, Detective. Take your cell phone out with one hand and toss it out the window. I'm not about to risk getting tracked."

Preston considered telling him that he didn't have one, but this wasn't the time to argue. He got rid of the phone.

Stan reached into Abby's purse next, feeling around for her phone and keeping his eyes on her and his gun out of reach. "If you both keep your cool, this will be over soon. Detective, you'll drive us out into the middle of nowhere, I'll drop both of you off, you catch the next ride into town and I keep going. No one needs to die."

They all heard Abby's phone beep just as he pulled it out. "Keep driving, Detective," he said, preempting any move from Preston with a wave of the gun toward Abby.

Stan glanced down at the text message. "That kid, Bobby, says he's decoded Carl's journal. He's ditched the guy watching him and is going to get the McCabe painting, 'The

Roundup.' Smart kid. He figured out where Carl hid it," he said. "Changing plans, folks. We're going to the ranch instead," he said, tossing the phone out the window and onto the bed of a passing pickup.

"You leave Bobby alone, Stan. He's just a kid," Abby said.

"Play by my rules and no one will die. You're talking with Crazyman, and I mean what I say," Stan said.

"So that was you sending those emails," Abby said.

"Of course. But I'm after the painting, not the kid," Stan added. "I take it and disappear, and you two go on with your lives."

Chapter Twenty-Four

"Why are you doing this, Stan? I still don't understand," Abby said.

"I grew up hearing all about Carl Sinclair and my grand-dad's fencing operations. Grandpa Miles got a little senile toward the end and Grandmother just assumed I'd think it was all crazy talk," Stan said. "For a long time I did. To me, Carl, the super thief, was just an arch villain/hero my granddad had made up. Then I met Ilse and new possibilities opened up."

"You knew that she'd bugged Rod's office?" Abby asked.

"Not at first. She and I became friends and one night I told her that I'd never meant to become an accountant. I'd wanted a life filled with excitement and adventure like my grand-dad's. When she heard the name Carl Sinclair, she said that he was back in town and told me what she'd overheard—Carl admitting that he'd changed his name. That's when I knew fate had given me a chance. Everything I'd ever wanted was right there just waiting for me to take it."

"So you convinced Ilse to help?" Preston asked him.

"It didn't take much convincing. Initially, she'd hoped to get something on Rod and blackmail him, but we both realized that we'd stumbled onto something much bigger. The paintings that Granddad and Carl had stolen were worth enough to keep us sipping mojitos in the Caribbean for the rest of our lives. We looked for them around the ranch on our own at first. Well, actually, I did while Ilse kept the chief's son distracted. He was always there till late. I wasn't able to find what we wanted, so we went to Plan B."

"You killed him because he refused to tell you?" Preston asked.

"No, man. It was self-defense. We tried to force him to tell us where he'd put the stuff by threatening to kill Bobby and making it look as if he'd done it if he didn't cooperate. He took us to Hank's enclosure, then came at me with a shovel. I wrenched it away from him, and while we were fighting, Ilse picked it up and hit him twice. He went down and stayed down—permanently."

"No one saw you two?" Preston asked.

"No, but that idiot camel wouldn't shut up. He started bellowing like crazy. Lucky for me it was thundering and nobody heard. Then we saw Monroe walking toward the enclosure. Ilse went to meet him and kept him busy, as usual, while I took care of things. I moved Carl's body as fast as I could, hoping that would get Hank to shut up. It did. He quieted down once he couldn't see Carl anymore. I left Carl's body in the horse pen, figuring people would assume the horses had spooked because of the storm and trampled Carl."

"You're not going to get away with this, Stan. Too many people know what you've done," Abby said.

"You also left Ilse standing there in handcuffs, so she'll probably say *you* were the one who hit Carl," Preston added.

"Doesn't matter. I've always had an escape plan. In a few hours I'll have disappeared forever. It's a funny thing about being an accountant. You make friends with all kinds of people, particularly if you're willing to break a few rules."

"Once you have the painting, you'll let us go?" Abby's voice shook, betraying her fear.

"I'll keep you with me until I'm out of town—insurance, if you will. After that, you're on your own."

PRESTON DROVE DIRECTLY to the ranch. He'd left Kyle with Bobby, and the chances of having the kid give his brother the slip for more than a minute or two were zero to none. Sure enough, as Preston pulled up, Kyle and Bobby were standing close by.

"Don't even think of doing something stupid, Detective," Stan said. "If you signal your brother, Abby's brains will be splattered all over the backseat."

Preston knew he wouldn't have to do anything at all. Though Kyle clearly hadn't been told about the situation yet, seeing him driving Stan's truck and sitting up front alone while Abby and Stan were in the back would flag his brother that something was wrong.

Preston climbed down out of the extended-cab four-door pickup as Stan and Abby came out the back. As they did, Preston saw Kyle's shoulder stiffen, then he bent down to talk to Bobby, who was holding something in his hand.

In an instant, Stan pushed Abby out in front of him and allowed Kyle to see his gun.

"If you make the wrong move the woman goes first, the boy second. You get me?" Stan growled.

Bobby froze, his eyes as big as saucers. "That's why two people were riding in the backseat."

Knowing Bobby had spent practically all his life pretending to be a spy, and worried he'd do something foolish with the wrench he was holding, Preston spoke quickly. "Bobby, we're going to be fine, so just do as Stan says."

Bobby nodded and swallowed hard.

"All right then. We're all on the same page," Stan said. "Kyle, put your weapon on the ground along with your radio and cell phone."

Kyle did as he was told, but the look on his face told Preston that he'd take the first available opportunity to rip Stan Cooper apart.

"Give me your handcuffs, Bowman," Stan ordered.

Preston hesitated. He knew what was coming next.

"Do it! Toss them to your brother," Stan ordered, pointing his pistol at Abby.

Preston removed them from the keeper on his belt and tossed them to Kyle. "Sorry, bro."

"Attach yourself to the bumper grill by your right wrist. One of those big bars, so you can't twist it loose," Stan ordered Kyle.

"No," Kyle said.

"Don't push me," Stan said, grabbing Abby and moving the gun under her chin.

Abby closed her eyes.

"All right," Kyle said. "Relax."

Kyle walked past Preston and Abby slowly, and as he did, he met his brother's eyes.

Preston knew that Kyle wanted nothing more than to tackle Stan, but he'd do what had to be done.

After Kyle had attached the handcuff to the big metal grill protector, Stan added, "Now your wrist."

Once Stan heard the click, he went over and took a closer look, keeping out of range of Kyle's arms and feet. "Okay, kid," he said, looking at Bobby. "You said you knew where the painting was. Where is it?"

"I sent the text to Abby, not you," Bobby said, his voice shaky. "Carl wouldn't have wanted you to have it."

"Look, kid, it's a trade. You give me the painting. Your friend Abby and her cop friend stay alive."

"Bobby, do as he says," Preston said.

"It's down there," Bobby said, pointing toward the animal pens.

"Lead the way," Stan said.

Bobby walked toward the barn even more slowly than usual. "The fence post by Hank's enclosure isn't like the other ones. It's hollow. Kyle and I had to go back to get a wrench so we could unscrew it. The top part is hard to move." Bobby held out the pipe wrench.

Preston was already trying to figure out a way to get to it. The wrench wasn't much of a weapon against a gun, but it would extend his reach enough to knock it away.

The one ace in the hole he still had was that Stan didn't know about the new cameras and Daniel, or one of his employees, had undoubtedly monitored their arrival. They'd have plenty of backup soon. All he had to do right now was stall for time and, if possible, try to get the drop on Stan before he did something stupid.

As they reached the enclosure, Hank began to bellow.

"Abby, make that thing shut up," Stan hissed.

"I can't. He won't listen. He hates you. You killed his friend," Abby said.

"I told you it was Ilse. Which post, kid?" Stan asked, keeping his gun on Abby, who was on his right.

"It's the one with the sign telling about Hank," Bobby said. "The sign is attached to a nut screwed into the top of the post."

"All right, kid. Use the wrench to take off the nut," he said.

Bobby tried, but it wouldn't move. "I'm not strong enough, even with the wrench. It's rusty and stuck. You have to do it."

"If you're pulling something, kid…" Stan said, his voice turning deadly.

"I'm not!"

"If that painting isn't there…"

"Carl said it would be!" He tapped the side of another pipe with the wrench and there was a solid metallic sound. Then he tapped the pipe holding the sign. "Listen," Bobby said. "Hear it? Sounds hollow, right? This is where he put it."

"Leave the wrench on the ground, Bobby," Stan said, then looked at Preston. "The kid must have loosened it up a little. Try it with your hands. *Don't* touch that wrench."

It took Preston a few seconds, but he was finally able to work the top loose. A thin wire led down the hollow pipe. Preston pointed it out and stepped back. "Go ahead."

All he needed was for Stan to move away from Abby. The second he reached over to pull out what was attached to the wire, he'd have him.

Almost as if reading his mind, Stan shook his head. "No, you pull it out for me, Bowman."

Working carefully, Preston grabbed the wire and pulled. The wire was connected to a cap attached to a smaller-diameter piece of white plastic pipe.

"Pop that cap off and let's see what's inside," Stan said, looking out of the corner of his eye toward Hank. The camel had come over to investigate.

Preston worked the cap loose. Inside was a rolled-up canvas painting held together by a string.

"Open it carefully. I want to make sure it's the real thing," Stan said.

"I'll need to reach for my pocket knife to cut the string," Preston said.

"Don't even think it. Slide the twine off."

Preston worked the string loose, then unrolled the canvas. He'd expected to see a scene from a roundup, but this had nothing to do with cowboys or cattle. It was almost a replica of the sketch *Hosteen* Silver had left for him. It depicted a small bird of prey protecting its nest from a large owl. Only one element was new to him, and it rocked him to the core. In the canyon below, a young boy watched the sky and a woman kneeled beside him. A single blue feather drifted down toward them, though neither seemed aware of it.

As Preston stared at the painting in his hands he knew destiny had found him.

"Aim it toward me so I can get a better look, but keep it away from the fence. I don't trust that camel."

Preston, still searching for an advantage, held the painting so Stan would have to turn his head slightly.

"It's not 'The Roundup,' but that painting's worth twice as much," he said. "It's titled 'Dreams' and is one of his earlier works. Roll it back up."

Preston did, working slowly to buy time.

"Looks like we're all coming out ahead on this. Even you, Abby," Stan said.

"What are you talking about, you weasel? I may lose the ranch."

"Cheer up. You're not as bad off as you think. I've been cooking the books ever since I found out about Carl. How else could I buy you out cheap? You're not rich, but you're definitely in the black. The same goes for Garner. I had to make sure he didn't try riding to your rescue, so I made him think he'd taken some heavy investment losses. Guess you both need to find a better accountant."

"She trusted you," Bobby said angrily.

"Live and learn, kid." Stan glanced at Preston. "Quit stalling and hand me the painting."

Holding out his left hand, Stan poked the barrel of his gun hard into Abby's ribs.

When Abby groaned, Bobby, who'd picked up the wrench unnoticed, smashed it against Stan's knee.

With a cry, Stan swung the pistol around toward Bobby, but Preston grabbed Stan's gun hand at the wrist, shoving it up and back and cracking the man's forehead with his own weapon.

The gun went off, sending a bullet into the sky.

Preston grabbed the pistol, tore it from Stan's grasp and kicked the man in the groin.

Slammed backward, Stan grunted in pain and fell to his knees. As he sagged against the fence rail, Hank brought his head down and bit Stan hard in the shoulder.

Stan cried out and rose to his feet, but Preston, having put the pistol on safe and tossing it aside, moved in. He threw a right cross that connected with Stan's jaw and sent the man tumbling back down to the ground.

Preston wanted this fight. "Get up. You're brave when you're holding a gun on a woman and a kid. Now let's see what you've got when you're fighting someone your own size."

Stan shook his head and stayed on the ground. "Forget it," he said, seeing Kyle and Daniel running up and hearing the wail of approaching police cars.

"I've got him," Preston called out, spinning Stan around and cuffing him with a zip tie, one of several he'd recently put in his pocket.

Abby retrieved Preston's pistol and stepped back with Bobby.

"We'll keep an eye on him for you until the officers arrive," Daniel said, moving Stan away from Abby and Bobby. "Go take care of your friends, bro."

Bobby grinned as Preston came up. "Way to go! I knew we could take him."

Preston looked at the boy and smiled. "And we did, buddy. Teamwork."

Bobby glanced back at Stan as Kyle and Daniel held him away from them. "You, me and Abby. We backed each other up when it counted, just like family."

"You've got that right," Preston said and bumped fists with Bobby. "That painting is still on the ground over there. You wanna get it before Hank does?"

"Sure." As Bobby hurried away, Preston focused on Abby. "He's right, you know," he murmured, pulling her into his arms. "The three of us are family in all the ways that count. Listen to White Wolf's call. Marry me, Abby. After that, we can adopt Bobby and make it official."

She smiled. "A package deal. What more could a woman want?"

"Let me give you a few ideas," he said and covered her mouth in a deep, slow kiss.

"About time," Bobby called out. "Grown-ups take *forever* to see what's right in front of them."

"Just plain stubbornness, if you ask me," Daniel said, laughing.

Epilogue

The cliffs were bathed in the gold, orange and red of late afternoon as Preston and Abby arrived at Copper Canyon. Moments after they parked, first Bobby came out of the house followed by Preston's brothers and two women Abby hadn't yet met.

"This is our last get-together before Kyle leaves again," Preston said.

"Is he coming back?" she asked.

Preston nodded. "By the end of the year. Now come meet some of the family."

Preston introduced Abby to Holly, Daniel's very pregnant wife, and then Gene introduced his wife, Lori.

Before Abby and Bobby could go into the house with the others, Preston took them aside. "I'd like to show both of you a very special place. It was where I first learned about being in a family."

Preston took Abby by the hand and led her and Bobby a little ways up the canyon.

"When *Hosteen* Silver first brought me here to Copper Canyon I had a rough time of it. Life hadn't taught me to trust anyone, so I didn't want to hang out with my brothers. I wanted a space of my own. A tree house seemed perfect. I'd seen one on TV, so I picked out that tree," he said, pointing to a large cottonwood next to the arroyo.

"You built that?" Bobby asked, looking up at the small four-sided boxlike structure.

"Not completely, no," Preston said.

"My idea at the time was just to put in some kind of floor and maybe a length of rope so I could climb up, but I couldn't do any of it alone. The more I tried, the more frustrated I got. One day after I had stormed off, ready to sulk, I looked back and saw Kyle and Gene starting to work together on the place. They were doing what I hadn't been able to do by myself. I went back and joined them. We all shared the work from that day on, and it turned out to be a great place. We used it for a long time."

"I try to do stuff alone, too," Bobby said. "It's hard to count on anyone else."

"My brothers and I aren't related by blood, but we're family in all the ways that matter most, like it is with Abby, you and me," Preston said. "So, Bobby, what do you say? Would you like to make it official?"

"You mean you'll foster me?" Bobby asked, his voice rising in excitement.

"No, I was thinking we could start the adoption process once Abby and I are married," Preston said.

"And we'll live in the big house at Sitting Tall Ranch," she said, "though we're going to have to do some remodeling."

"And lots of repainting," Preston said with a grin.

"More blue?" she said, laughing. "What color do you want your room to be, Bobby?"

"My own family *and* my own room? Who cares what color it is," he said.

"Okay," Preston said. "Now that we've got that settled, let's go back to the house. Kyle's got everything we need, Bobby, including a baseball glove that needs to be broken in. While we're waiting for dinner, you and I can go practice throwing and catching and maybe take a few swings with the bat."

"For real?" Bobby asked.

"For real," Preston said with a smile.

"Can I get in on that?" Abby asked.

"Hey, you're part of the family team now, too—the Copper Canyon crew. We're unstoppable."

As they headed back, Bobby leading the way, Preston placed his arm around Abby's waist and pulled her closer to his side.

Abby looked up at him and smiled. "So what do we do for a second date, Detective Bowman?"

"Get married? I've got this ring in my pocket...."

* * * * *

COMING NEXT MONTH from Harlequin® Intrigue®
AVAILABLE AUGUST 20, 2013

#1443 BRIDAL ARMOR
Colby Agency: The Specialists
Debra Webb
Thomas Casey's extreme black ops team is the best at recovering the worst situations. When thrust into the most dangerous situation of his career, can he recover his heart?

#1444 TASK FORCE BRIDE
The Precinct: Task Force
Julie Miller
A tough K-9 cop masquerades as the fiancé of a shy bridal-shop owner in order to protect her from the terrifying criminal who's hot on her trail.

#1445 GLITTER AND GUNFIRE
Shadow Agents
Cynthia Eden
Cale Lane is used to life-or-death battles. But when the former army ranger's new mission is to simply watch over gorgeous socialite Cassidy Sherridan, he follows orders.

#1446 BODYGUARD UNDER FIRE
Covert Cowboys, Inc.
Elle James
Recruited to join an elite undercover group, former army Special Forces soldier Chuck Bolton returns to Texas. And his first assignment is to protect his former fiancé...and the child he's never met.

#1447 THE BETRAYED
Mystere Parish: Family Inheritance
Jana DeLeon
Danae LeBeau thought she'd find answers when she returned to her childhood home, but someone doesn't like the questions she's asking. And the guy next door will stop at nothing to find out why.

#1448 MOST ELIGIBLE SPY
HQ: Texas
Dana Marton
After being betrayed by her own brother, can Molly Rogers trust an unknown soldier to save her and her son from ruthless smugglers who are out for blood?

You can find more information on upcoming Harlequin® titles, free excerpts and more at www.Harlequin.com.

HICNM0813

REQUEST YOUR FREE BOOKS!
2 FREE NOVELS PLUS 2 FREE GIFTS!

ᕼ HARLEQUIN®

INTRIGUE®

BREATHTAKING ROMANTIC SUSPENSE

YES! Please send me 2 FREE Harlequin Intrigue® novels and my 2 FREE gifts (gifts are worth about $10). After receiving them, if I don't wish to receive any more books, I can return the shipping statement marked "cancel." If I don't cancel, I will receive 6 brand-new novels every month and be billed just $4.74 per book in the U.S. or $5.24 per book in Canada. That's a savings of at least 14% off the cover price! It's quite a bargain! Shipping and handling is just 50¢ per book in the U.S. and 75¢ per book in Canada.* I understand that accepting the 2 free books and gifts places me under no obligation to buy anything. I can always return a shipment and cancel at any time. Even if I never buy another book, the two free books and gifts are mine to keep forever.

182/382 HDN F42N

Name _____ (PLEASE PRINT) _____

Address _____ Apt. # _____

City _____ State/Prov. _____ Zip/Postal Code _____

Signature (if under 18, a parent or guardian must sign) _____

Mail to the Harlequin® Reader Service:
IN U.S.A.: P.O. Box 1867, Buffalo, NY 14240-1867
IN CANADA: P.O. Box 609, Fort Erie, Ontario L2A 5X3

**Are you a subscriber to Harlequin Intrigue books
and want to receive the larger-print edition?
Call 1-800-873-8635 or visit www.ReaderService.com.**

* Terms and prices subject to change without notice. Prices do not include applicable taxes. Sales tax applicable in N.Y. Canadian residents will be charged applicable taxes. Offer not valid in Quebec. This offer is limited to one order per household. Not valid for current subscribers to Harlequin Intrigue books. All orders subject to credit approval. Credit or debit balances in a customer's account(s) may be offset by any other outstanding balance owed by or to the customer. Please allow 4 to 6 weeks for delivery. Offer available while quantities last.

Your Privacy—The Harlequin® Reader Service is committed to protecting your privacy. Our Privacy Policy is available online at www.ReaderService.com or upon request from the Harlequin Reader Service.

We make a portion of our mailing list available to reputable third parties that offer products we believe may interest you. If you prefer that we not exchange your name with third parties, or if you wish to clarify or modify your communication preferences, please visit us at www.ReaderService.com/consumerchoice or write to us at Harlequin Reader Service Preference Service, P.O. Box 9062, Buffalo, NY 14269. Include your complete name and address.

HI13R